ARPress
45 Dan Road Suite 36
Canton MA 02021

Hotline: 1(800) 220-7660
Fax: 1(855) 752-6001

Ordering Information:
Quantity sales. Special discounts are available on quantity purchases by corporations, associations, and others. For details, contact the publisher at the address above.

Printed in the United States of America.

ISBN-13:   Paperback   979-8-89676-004-7
                 eBook   979-8-89676-005-4

Library of Congress Control Number: 2024925142

PROLOGUE

ADRI WAS SITTING BY THE POOL WHEN SHE LOOKED UP FROM THE BOOK SHE WAS READING. She could see a man standing in the Glassed-In Dining Room on the second floor. The dining room had floor to ceiling windows looking down over the pool. He looked angry—the only people at the pool were herself and Emmy. Emmy was a cute and smart four-year-old. This last week Emmy had spent a lot of time with Adri's granddaughters Ally and Lisa. Adri's son and his family had left early this morning. Adri had rented the suite for the rest of the week. Her plane wasn't leaving until Sunday. Adri had come down to the pool to watch over Emmy.

She looked up, and the mad man was standing at the pool's edge. He started yelling for Emmy to get out of the pool. Emmy said. "Look, Papa, I can swim." He continued loudly, "Where is your Mother? You shouldn't be swimming alone".

Emmy said, "I'm not swimming alone. Look Papa what I can do". Emmy went into a jellyfish float. The angry man said, "Does your Mother know you are at the pool"? Emmy came up from the water. She hadn't heard her Papa. He said, "Get out of the pool. You arc not to be swimming alone". Emmy said, "I'm not swimming alone, Adri is watching me." He turned his angry eyes at Adri and said, "Who are you and why are you watching my granddaughter"? "Where is her mother"?

Adri had waited all week to say something about Emmy being left alone everyday all day. Adri said, "That is a good question. I would like to know where her mother is as well". We have looked for her and left notes for her all week". Emmy has been enjoying this week by hooking up with my granddaughters and even though they left this morning. I came down to the pool at 9 am to watch Emmy because no one else has all week". He said to Emmy, "Where is your Mother?" Adri said, "I just told you we don't know and haven't known all week. She leaves every morning telling Emmy she is in work out room, she has never been there all week". The man said, "Where is sissy, who is feeding her and taking care of her." Adri had enough, "Sir, I'm trying to tell you Emmy has been on her own all week. She takes care of the puppy at 11:00 am and 2 pm. She is very responsible". He finally turned to Adri and said. "She doesn't know how to tell time, and we don't have a puppy." Adri said, "Then who is sissy"? He said, "Her baby sister"! Adri jumped up and said. "Emmy let's get going to check on Sissy." They all three hurriedly went to the patio door, of the ground floor suite, and Emmy got a key out from under the rock and let them in. She said, "Is it already 11 am"? Adri said, "Emmy can you show your Papa and I how you take care of Sissy"? Emmy said, "Sure." She led them through a living area that looked like someone must have had a party and not cleaned up. Then they went into a room that not only looked like a tornado had been through but smelled like a toilet.

Emmy went over to the baby crib; the side of the crib was down. She awoke sissy, and they giggled together, well the baby didn't giggle, but you could tell she was happy. Emmy changed the baby's diaper, like a professional. She used baby wipes and cleaned her sister. She put powder on her sissy and then a clean diaper. Then she went over to a sack and got out a package of formula in small bottles. She opened the package and took one to the microwave, shaking it all the way. She then heated the bottle. Adri didn't notice how long, she had been looking around the room. Emmy picked up Sissy and sat down on the bed and started feeding her. Adri said, "Emmy while you feed Sissy, your Papa and I are going to talk." "Emmy, you are a great big sister." "Who showed you how to take care of Sissy"? Emmy said, "I googled it."

Chapter 1

ADRI NOW LOOKED ANGRY AT EMMY'S PAPA. She said, "Before we talk, I would like for you to go check the messages at the desk for this suite." He walked out. Emmy walked into the room, still feeding the baby. She said, "Is my Papa mad at me"? It broke Adri's heart. Adri said, "No, he is not mad at you. He is just busy trying to figure something out". "You have done an excellent job of taking care of your Sissy, and I'm proud of you." Adri had been mad all week that a Mother would leave her four year old alone all day. Now Adri was seeing red! Emmy's Papa walked back into the room. Emmy said, "Now I have to burp Sissy and put her back in bed."

The minute Emmy was in the adjoining room, Adri said, "Who and where are these girls' mother"? Emmy's Papa said, "Her mother is here every day when I get into the room about 5:30 or 6:00. I just assumed they had been together all day because of all the things Emmy was talking about she had done that day. Then within 30 minutes, her mother would head out for a night on the town, and I would watch the girls. I'm so furious that I truly see red". "What is that smell"? Adri answered, "Could be something in this mess, but I guess that Emmy has wet the bed, and no one has changed it and the baby also has wet her crib, but Emmy put a towel under her." Her Papa said, "Thank you for watching my granddaughter this week. You probably saved her life or worse."

"I brought my stepdaughter on this business trip because I thought she and her girls could enjoy a mini-vacation together. Now I find she has been leaving them during the day and going only God knows where. She is then running in to change for a night on the town. I don't know how to express my appreciation. I am truly sorry for my first impression. I need to apologize to Emmy as well as you. Now I still have a problem, I'm closing on a multi-million-dollar deal, and I need someone to watch Emmy and Sissy". Adri said, "I'll take care of them. You go back to your meetings". Before he left Emmy's Papa said, "When I looked out the dining room window and saw Emmy alone in the swimming pool. I was frightened, frightened more than when I was serving in the military. I knew she couldn't swim. Now, I feel like I'm shaking inside thinking about what all could have happened to Emmy this week". "I'm so sorry I reacted to you the way I did, I can never repay what you did for me this week." Adri said, "I'm just glad it is all in the open and can now be resolved." "By the way, my name is Adri." Emmy's Papa put his hand out and said, "My name is Cord."

Adri said, "I've got this handled, go and close your deal." Cord was furious at his stepdaughter. He made one call before he left the suite. He called his attorney Jake. Jake would know how to proceed with his stepdaughter. Then he headed back to the conference center. He needed to get this deal closed before he could deal with her. The minute Cord walked back into the conference room, and his mind shifted to all business.

The minute Cord walked out of the suite; Adri got moving. Emmy was still in the bedroom. Adri went in the bathroom and moved enough out of the way to run a bath for Emmy. There were no clean towels, and she ran across to Cord's suite to get a towel. It was like going from a tornado sight into a Church. Cords room had everything in place. "Good", she ran into the bathroom and grabbed a washcloth and a towel. She ran back to Emmy, who was playing in the bathtub. What a good child, too bad she didn't have a Mother to speak of.

Adri called room service and ordered Mac and Cheese and a chocolate Sunday for Emmy. This had been their routine all week when Emmy was with her granddaughters, and she thought it best to follow the routine. Adri then called the front desk and asked to speak with the manager.

Adri asked the manager of the resort if she could send up two housekeepers and that she would need them for an hour to two hours. She arranged for the service to be added to the bill along with a 20% tip for each lady. The ladies arrived before Emmy's food. Adri asks the ladies to change both beds in Emmy's room and the sheets in the crib. Adri explained that all the bedding needed to be changed. Adri also told the ladies to replace the towel and the washcloth in the other bath and give that bedroom the white glove. After that to start in the living area. She knew the women should be going home about this time, so they had either volunteered or were told to stay over. Adri felt bad about that, so she told the ladies that a 20% tip had been added to the amount she was paying for this service. She told them it was 20% for each lady. Then Adri said she didn't know how the resort would handle that tip, so she handed each lady a $50 bill and said now I know you will be compensated for this extra work. They were excellent. They worked together and had the beds redone with all clean linens before Emmy was out of the bath. Adri went into the bathroom and helped Emmy wash her hair and complete her bath. Emmy had long curly hair, so Adri parted it off and braided five braids on top and five braids on bottom. Emmy got in clean comfy pajamas and propped herself up in one of the clean beds. Adri brought her Mac and Cheese and put her Sunday in the Suite refrigerator. The ladies brought in a new crib mattress, and while they changed out the mattress and sheets, Adri took Sissy and bathed her. When she was finished Adri put a clean diaper on Sissy with a clean onesie. Emmy was ready for her Ice cream Sunday and Adri brought it to her and removed the empty Mac and Cheese bowl. Now that the girls were settled Adri started picking up the bedroom. She piled all the toys in one pile, all the trash in another, all the dirty clothes in another. As she was organizing the room where the ladies would be able to clean, she noticed that some of the clothes on the floor and the furniture still had sales tags on them. Those clothes, Adri hung up and was careful not to throw away any receipts as well. Adri ran into the living room, and the ladies had finished the other bedroom and were cleaning in there. Adri asks them if they found any receipts to please save them. Adri grabbed an arm full of toys the ladies had stacked and went back for another arm full of dirty clothes. These clothes were mostly ladies. For never being there, this woman sure went through a lot of clothes. Adri asks the ladies to watch the girls, they were both asleep because she was running to the gift shop. They were happy to oblige. Adri was back in three minutes. She had gotten two net hampers shaped likes frogs to put all the toys in. In Adri's organizing, she found five sacks of clothing that were still new in the sacks. The clothes had never even been gotten out of the sacks much less worn. The tickets were miraculously still in the sacks. Adri put the sacks in the closet. She was thinking 'if Cord was mad, he might not feel so generous.' There were no new clothes for Sissy or Emmy. That just made Adri more upset.

Adri moved the Baby Crib over by one of the dressers and made the dresser top into a diaper table. She opened the top drawer and organized all the supplies in it. Then she took the sack of bottles and organized them by the microwave. The ladies were now ready to move into the bedroom with the two girls. They started with the bathroom, and once again, Adri asks if they would watch the girls while she ran to the gift shop. They eagerly agreed. Before she left the suite, she realized they had been vacuuming, and it had not bothered either of the girls, so she told them to go ahead and vacuum when they got to that point.

Adri literally ran to the gift shop and bought all the baby things and all the clothes that were size 3 or 4. Emmy was probably a size three even though she was four she was small. She bought blankets, pajamas, everything she spotted that they might need. She asks them to charge it to the suite and deliver it as soon as possible. They were pleased to deliver or so they said. Adri ran back to the suite, and the ladies were still busy working. They were not missing anything. They were excellent. Several loads of laundry had accumulated, and Adri couldn't figure out how she would handle the laundry. Adri asks the ladies for some extra trash bags, and she sorted the laundry and put the different loads into the trash bags. She put them on the bed that Emmy was not sleeping in.

The ladies finished the bedroom and asked Adri if she wanted to hold the baby while they vacuumed. Adri fixed a bottle and went over and got Sissy out of the crib, changed her diaper. Then took her in the living room to feed her. Sissy was sleeping in Adri's arms when the ladies ask for Adri to walk through each room and see if there was anything left undone. Adri had been watching the ladies closely and knew the suite looked brand new. She walked through and complimented the ladies. One of the ladies asks if she wanted them to do the laundry. She said, "That is a service we offer, and in this case, we will do it ourselves and get it right back to you. Adri was thankful. She told the ladies to bill the laundry to the suite and add a 20% tip. Then she went to her purse and got out two more $50 bills and gave each one. She said, "The manager gave me the best when she sent you two. Thank you so much, plus I hope you also get the 20% tip, but I don't have any control over that". The ladies left with the laundry.

Adri was enjoying holding Sissy when someone knocked. It was the gift shop. They had taken all the tags off and folded the clothes as Adri had requested. Adri signed the ticket and took the clothes to the girls' bedroom. She opened drawers and put the clothes up. The baby's clothes and things fit perfectly in the other two drawers under the supply drawer Adri had fixed earlier. Adri put Emmy's clothes in drawers beside Sissy's. Where were the suitcases? Adri just realized that there were no suitcases in the room. She picked Sissy back up and went into the living area.

Then someone started trying to get in the door. Adri was thinking, what will I do if it is their mother. When Cord walked in, he stood in shock! He finally said, "If I didn't see you holding Sissy, I would have thought I was in the wrong suite." "Thank God, you have taken care of all this." Adri said, "Care to see the girls' room." Adri could tell Cord was very pleased. Emmy was still fast asleep. Cord said, "I came back on the break because I heard from my stepdaughter. She has plans to sail away with some stranger, that she is calling her soul mate. Lucky for me the Port Master won't allow them to leave Port until in the morning. I have contacted my attorney, and he has contacted a local attorney to take care of all the paperwork. The sum of it is that Emmy's Daddy and his wife will be here to pick up Emmy between 5 and 5:30. I will be out of my meeting by then. Is it possible for you to pack up Emmy and have her ready? Well, I know it's possible I need to know if you will help me out". Adri nodded her head, yes. As Cord continued, "The Attorney will also be here with the papers hopefully that my stepdaughter has signed giving full custody to Emmy's Dad and signing custody of Sissy over to me." Cord added. 'Thank you, and I've got to run". Adri yelled, "Good Luck."

Amy called the gift shop, identified herself, and ask if they had any luggage appropriate for a child. They said yes, they would bring the pieces to the suite where she could see what she would like. They were at the door in less than ten minutes. She knew how much she bought, plus what she had seen in the laundry, and the little in the drawers before the shopping spree. She picks two pieces, the large and the medium bags in pink polka dot. She opened the bags on the other bed and laid one outfit for Emmy to wear and started packing. While she was packing, the ladies brought the laundry back all folded. Adri told them what a luxury they had been and how pleased she was and thanked them again before they left. Adri finished packing Emmy's things and put the two pink polka dot suitcases in the living room by the door. She also put the two net frogs full of toys with the bags

Adri just wanted to pick up Sissy and hold her, but Sissy was asleep, and she had more to prepare. Adri called dining services and ordered a tray of finger sandwiches, a vegetable tray with dip, and a tray of cookies. Plus tea, coffee, and water. She asks them to doll up the trays and drinks and bring service for 20. Adri was not expecting that many, but it would be supper time, and people may eat more than usual.

Then she went and picked up Sissy and set down to think. Adri had ordered the food for 4 pm, and she figured if you were finally getting the child you had wanted for four years, you would be early. Cord came back to the room at 3 pm.

He had a migraine headache; Adri knew just what to do. She asks him if he had any medicine and he told her, yes but he had taken it two days in a row, and the migraine had just rebounded. She made coffee and gave him a chocolate bar she had found with a lot of other candy. She had just put the candy in a cabinet earlier. Then she went to her purse. She knew his eyes and speech were already being affected. She told him to strip and get in bed. She hung up his clothes. She turned down the air conditioner a couple of degrees and closed all the blinds blacking out the room. Last, she asks him if he was allergic to codeine. He told her he wasn't. He had taken it before when he had a stress fracture. She gave him a Dramamine and a Tylenol with codeine. She said, "You should be asleep in the next fifteen minutes; if not, I'll give you another." "I'll also wake you when everyone has arrived."

Adri checked on Cord, and he was sound asleep, she shut his door. She propped the door to the suite open around 4 pm because she didn't want the waiting staff to knock and wake up Cord. They came with everything set up on a rolling cart that opened into a table. It was covered with a tablecloth, and everything looked beautiful. She signed the ticket added a tip, and they quietly left. She woke Emmy up and gave her a fruit cup. Emmy ate it while Adri finished drying her braids. Adri showed Emmy her new outfit, but Emmy ate another fruit cup before she started dressing. The outfit was adorable on Emmy and Adri had found a cute pair of sandals in all the rubble earlier. Adri started taking Emmy's braids out, and the curls and waves looked like a professional had styled her hair. Emmy had great hair.

Adri told Emmy that she had some news. Then she proceeded to tell her that her Daddy was coming to get her, and she would be living with them. Emmy said, "I always have lived with them, only when I visit my Papa. Sometimes when I visit my Papa, my Mommy is there, but my Mommy has a drug problem. Papa made her go to rehab while she was pregnant with Sissy, but after Sissy was born, she left the hospital and went right back to be with her druggy friends. My Mommy is not very responsible. I have to be responsible when I am with her. I never stay with her alone because my Papa and my Daddy are afraid something could happen to me. Papa thought she might be capable of taking care of me this week, but she hasn't been. I never know where she is, and

I have had to take care of Sissy myself". Wow, Adri thought, out of the mouth of babes. Emmy continued, "I like living at my Dads, my Mommy there is a First Grade Teacher. I will be in her First Grade in two more years. I love her, and I love my Dad. I don't really know my Mommy because she is never around". What a sad story but only Adri was sad. It was a fact of life for Emmy, and she had accepted it long ago.

Emmy was ready, and they had just walked into the living area when she saw the cookies. She was on her second when there was a knock on the door. It was her Daddy and her Step Mommy, which Emmy and everyone who knew them considered Emmy's Mommy. They were all three very happy, and Adri introduced herself. Emmy asks them if they would like a little sandwich or a cookie. She took them over to the table, and they each got a plate and something to drink. Adri said, "We are waiting for the attorney to arrive." When he arrives, I will wake up Cord, he has a migraine and is laying down". She was really hoping Cord would wake up on his own. If she had to wake him up, he might not get over his headache as quickly. She had just put that thought together, and Cord walked into the room. He must have taken a shower, he looked really good. She wondered what she looked like. She had touched up her makeup and brushed through her hair, but she felt frazzled by all that she had gone through today. She handed Cord a cup of coffee and ask him quietly if he thought he could eat a finger sandwich or a cookie. He told her he was feeling much better.

Chapter 2

AS SOON AS CORD CALLED HIS ATTORNEY JAKE, his attorney knew what to do. While Adri had been busy watching over the girls, he had been busy handling Debbie, and it wasn't the first time. He had dealt with Debbie many times. First, he contacted Cords security team, he knew they monitored her calls and Cords calls. He felt for sure they knew her location. Sure enough, they not only knew where she was, but they also had a team of four at the dock. Jake told them his plans and that he needed them to be present. Then Jake contacted a local attorney to make sure all the papers were drawn up according to the local and state requirements.

Jake arrived within the hour with a hairdresser, a makeup artist, a clothes designer, and a cameraman. When they boarded the boat, the security team boarded first. Jake explained to Debbie that the hairdresser, makeup artist and designer were all here for her. The cameraman would be filming. It was all about her. That was all Debbie heard. The team, that was to be working with Debbie had gotten their instructions from Jake. They were to make her look less like a junky. They were very good at their jobs. The designer dressed Debbie in an oversized starched shirt, baggie jeans, with a colorful, maxi length, silk Kimono draped over them. The appearance was very deceiving. The shirt and jeans filled out under the Colorful Kimono, Debbie lost her skeletal appearance. Debbie was sitting where the cameraman placed her. He put the soft light on her and with the combination of clean styled hair and pancake photo makeup, Debbie would pass the Judge's scrutiny.

The Judge, his Paralegal, and a notary were escorted on the boat right at that moment. Jake had all the legal papers organized and laid in order on the table in front of the Judge. The Judge introduced himself and ordered Cord's Attorney, Jake to proceed. The first order of business was to deal with the custody of Emmy. Debbie said she was happy to agree and, signed the papers. She was not interested in the standard visitation. She said, "if I want to visit, there has never been a problem." The Judge said, "So Ruled." The papers were then signed by the Judge, two witnesses and notarized.

Jake proceeded with the next order of business, which was concerning Ginger (sissy). Debbie wanted to say something. Jake thought fast and agreed knowing he could edit the recording later. Debbie began, "I did not and do not want this child. I told my stepfather this from the beginning, but because he does not believe in abortion. (Jake would delete that lie, Cord actually believed in a woman's right to choose, but Debbie's pregnancy passed the legal, due date for her to have an abortion) I was admitted to rehab until I delivered the child. I walked out of the hospital on the very same day of the delivery. I told the hospital staff then that the baby was now Cord's responsibility. They needed to contact him, which they did. Now I'm ready to sign the papers about custody and the papers about parental rights". The Judge said, "I don't need to hear anymore; you have made yourself very clear." Jake brought all the papers forward to be signed by the Judge first, then witnessed and notarized".

Chapter 3

WHILE CORD VISITED WITH EMMY'S PARENTS, Adri went into the bedroom and changed and fed Sissy. She heard the attorney arrive but stayed in the bedroom. She lay down on the bed with Sissy and was playing with her. She must be only a week old, maybe two. She was just beautiful. Adri had changed Sissy's outfit when she changed her diaper. She had that sweet baby smell. Adri hadn't realized that Cord had come into the room. He had been watching her and Sissy for a few minutes. He was thinking, what a beautiful sight. He finally spoke, "Adri, Emmy is fixing to leave if you would like to say goodbye." Adri answered, "I would like that." She picked up Sissy, and they walked into the living area together. Emmy's Dad thought, they really make a striking couple. Emmy had lots of hugs and kisses for Adri and lots of messages for Adri's granddaughters. Adri was really happy Emmy was going to live with her Dad.

Cord and Adri stood at the door and told them all goodbye. When they were gone, Adri turned to Cord and asked him how he was feeling. He said, "Like I could eat a steak." Adri said, "I always wake up from a migraine wanting steak and real French fries." Cord said, "Now that you mention it." They both burst out laughing as Cord picked up the phone and ordered them both steaks.

Adri still had Sissy in her arms. Cord was saying that he was supposed to be hosting his Chinese guest out on the town tonight but when he started having the migraine for the third day in a row. He called a company that specialized in that, and they had a Chinese Host they could send with the group instead of him going. I have to be very careful what I say that I don't insult them in any way. I never told the service I was ill. I said tonight is not for business tonight is for their pleasure. The host seemed pleased with what I said.

"I'm glad you decided to stay in". All those lights flashing in the club. Women wearing their heavy perfumes. "That wouldn't help your headache." They were both laughing at what she said. He knew she was teasing him. Adri said, "You know it doesn't seem like we just met this morning, it seems like we have known each other longer. I know this day had to have been a roller coaster of emotions for you. I felt caught up in it as well. By the way, what is Sissy's name"? Cord said, "Her name is Ginger." Adri said, "I like Ginger." Cord said, "I noticed every time I've seen you today you have been holding her. I got her mother to relinquish her parental rights and give me custody. But before I can adopt her, I have to find her father. The attorney took the DNA today of the guy she is sailing away with. He was so interested in becoming a Dad, that he signed away his parental rights before even finding our whether he was the father". Adri said, "That is better than having to pay him off. I guess he is one step up from the lowest". "Hopefully, he is the Dad, and you don't have to look any farther." "What I can't tolerate is these parents that go around telling everyone how great a parent they are when everyone in the room knows they aren't even raising their child." Cord said, "I agree."

Adri said, "Guess we are both emotionally drained. Maybe we should change the subject". "Were you able to complete your deal"? Cord answered, "Yes," as he was walking to answer the door. It was a dining service. The food smelled delicious. Adri thought that she always loved the smell of steak. Adri went into the bedroom and got a couple of blankets. She came back in the living area and made a little blanket bed for Ginger on one of the chairs closest to where the table was set for them to eat. They set down at the table, and Cord thanked God for watching over his granddaughters. The prayer was very moving, and when it was over, Adri wiped the tears out of her eyes.

Once they were eating, Adri said, "I signed a few tickets on your suite account today." Cord said, "Thank you. Thank you for taking care of my girls and taking care of the suite. I saw my stepdaughter, Debbie bringing in one shopping bag after another. I never dreamed that it was all for herself. That she bought nothing for her babies. Thank you for buying clothes for both girls." Hearing Emmy tell her parents all she did this week with your family. I felt guilty over leaving the girls in Debbie's care, or maybe I should say guilty over Debbie's neglect. The attorney videoed her statement relinquishing her parental rights. It should have been sad, but instead, I wanted to clap". Adri said, "There are many more parents who should relinquish their rights because the children are suffering and will continue to suffer. Emmy talked to me this afternoon about her mother. She has her eyes wide open about her mother. She also knows you and her Daddy agree. I was very impressed; cognitively her reasoning is above her age level. But kids taking adult responsibility early grow up reasoning earlier".

"Well, I keep getting off track. There are several sacks of new clothes in the closet. I only checked to see if the receipts were with them and that the receipts matched what was in the sacks. I wanted to suggest that the clothes be returned and credited back to I presume your account. I also picked up brand new clothes that still had the tags on them all over the room. I did find some receipts, but I haven't matched them to the clothes yet. If I can match the receipts than I would also suggest they be returned for credit". "I've been in your business a lot today, and you may be ready to send me to my room". Cord said, "Please don't even think that. I appreciate everything you have done for me today. If not for you, we may have never known Debbie was gone until after she had sailed away. You have treated both my granddaughters as if they were your own. Thank you for your generosity toward my family and myself. I talked to the desk, and they are transferring your charges for this week to my credit card. I would like for you to change your plans about leaving tomorrow and travel with me for the next couple of weeks. I will be staying at 5 Star Resorts, and I think you would enjoy them.

"I also would like you to watch over Ginger. I would also like to get to know you. I can already see that we have similar thinking on several different topics. If you will say yes, I will have your things moved into the suite tonight". Adri was surprised at his straightforward offer. She had been busy today and had not thought that her actions would lead to a proposal to travel with Cord. When she hesitated, Cord said, "The deal that I have been working on this week, is the same I will be offering to other investors. I have refined it this week, and now I am confident in my presentation, so I will be able to relax and enjoy more in the next two weeks." Adri answered, "I would love to spend more time with you and Ginger." Cord got up and went to the phone and made arrangements for her things to be moved to his suite. When they brought her things, he had them set her bags in the girls' suite.

When they were alone, Adri said, "How long will we be staying here"? Cord said, "I had planned on leaving the day after tomorrow. Is that alright with you"? Adri said, "I'm happy to be on your schedule now. I can return the clothes tomorrow if you want. Does Ginger have a car seat"? Cord answered, "Thank you for taking care of the clothes. Ginger's car seat is in the car. I have a car and driver here. What time do you plan on going out tomorrow"? Adri said, "I was thinking around 10 am unless you need the car". Cord said, "The driver will have the car out front at 10 am. I do not need the car so take as long as you like". Adri said, "Thank you if you don't need me for anything else tonight. It has been an exhausting day, and I'm going to bed". "Good night, Cord." "Goodnight, Adri."

Adri took care of putting Ginger to sleep. Then she stepped in a long hot bath and turned on the jets. She left the door open between the room and the bath in case Ginger made any sound she would be able to hear her. She was so exhausted she nearly fell asleep in the bathtub.

She got on some comfy pajamas and laughed because of the sexy man in the next room. She saw herself in the mirror and thought not the too sexy girl. So, she decided to go through receipts before she went to bed, and it was surprisingly easy to match everything up. Then she made a list of the stores that she would need to cover. She put them into the GPS and saw they were all very close in proximity.

She picked out her clothes for the next day and packed a diaper bag for Ginger. She picked an outfit for Ginger to wear, and she packed an outfit in the diaper bag. The diaper bag was first class, she guessed because it was for Debbie to carry. It was the first item Adri had found that could be considered for one of the kids. Adri also looked for a Children's Store in that same area. Then she got in bed and closed her eyes. Ginger only woke her up once during the night. Adri changed her and fed her, and then they both went back to sleep.

The car and driver were waiting for Adri when she got to the lobby. He introduced himself to Adri. His name was Marion. She told him to call her Adri, and the baby's name is Ginger. He had loaded her sacks in the trunk. When he got into the limousine, Adri said, "I need to return the items in the sacks. I have made a list of the stores that I need to go to take care of it". She showed him her GPS, and he said, "I know just where you are going." "I drove Debbie the day she went shopping."

They started on their way, and Adri said, "I really don't know how long this will take, but I would also like to go to a couple of children stores in the area." Marion said, "That's a fine idea, you sure have Ginger dolled up pretty today." Adri said, "I was fortunate that the gift shop had a couple of baby outfits."

Marion had been driving with Cord for 11 years. He was impressed with Adri. When Cord had called him last night, he had told him all Adri had accomplished yesterday, and he also told him about her taking care of Emmy all last week. Marion was glad that Cord was finally opening his life to a beautiful women with intelligence. Marion knew how hurt Cord had been by his wife when she left with another man. He also knew how much time and money Cord had spent trying to get that stepdaughter of his straightened out. Cord would have been better off if Debbie had left with her mother. The best thing about Debbie staying with Cord was those two little ones. Marion had seen Emmy grow up over these last four years, and now he was looking forward to watching Ginger as she grew up. He wanted the best for both of these baby girls.

They arrived at the first shop and while Adri got Ginger out of her car seat. Marion got the bags out of the back that he could see were from this store. He opened the door for Adri and Ginger then he took the sacks and put them on the counter. He told Adri he would wait at the car. As he was walking to the door, he heard Adri say, "I need to return these items." As she was handing the receipt to the clerk. The clerk was a little snooty she said, "Was anything wrong with the items"? Adri said sweetly, "No, they are perfectly beautiful, but the girl that bought them has sailed off with her lover." The clerk's manner changed, and they were laughing when Marion left the shop. Marion was thinking, and I think I'm falling in love with this lady.

When Adri came out of the shop, Marion opened her door. Adri said, "Marion, it is such a beautiful day. I think I'll walk the shop is just next door, it was a half a block walk". Marion got the next sacks and walked with Adri to the next store. He opened the door to the shop for Adri and Ginger and placed the sacks on the counter, he went directly back to the car and moved it to the front of the shop. He was moving it, where it would be convenient for Adri but also because he knew how snooty these shop girls could be and he knew seeing the limousine and driver might help in how they treated Adri. They seemed to cater to money.

Adri came out and thanked Marion for moving the limousine. She got in, and they drove a couple of blocks to the next store. Marion could tell Adri was excited she finally couldn't contain herself. She said, "You know I don't like doing this. I could hardly sleep thinking about returning these clothes. I'm sure these shop keepers do not like losing a sale of this amount". She continued, "I can sympathize with them, but it sure is fun when they credit Cord's account with all that money. It is now up to 112,000 dollars. A lot of the clothes I found just thrown on the floor. I sure hope Debbie's lover knows what a spender she has been". "I'm sorry I probably shouldn't be talking about Cord's business, but I couldn't contain myself." Marion said, "You didn't tell me anything I didn't already know. I've been working for Cord for a lot of years. I travel with him, and we rent a car locally. Cord this decided years ago because he likes someone hc can depend on. He is a very generous employer and friend".

They had arrived at the next shop. Adri thanked Marion for visiting with her. She took Ginger out of her car seat and changed her. She asked Marion if he thought they would be able to park here long enough for her to feed Ginger. Marion told her to take her time, and if he needed to move the car, he would drive around the block. Adri fed Ginger and burped her. The whole time she was talking softly to Ginger. When she was ready, Marion got the sacks and came around to open the door. They followed their pattern at two more shops. Then Marion stopped in front of a children's shop.

Adri lit up, and she said, "Thank you, Marion. This is just what I needed to pick me up. It's a little depressing to beg for your money back. This will be great fun"! Marion said, "You girls have fun. I'm assuming you have Cord's credit card"?

Adri said, "No, but I have plenty of money of my own." "I like making my own decisions if I had needed money, I would have talked to him, but then I would have been accountable to him for my decisions." Marion said, "You are surely different from the other women he has had in his life." Adri got out of the limousine laughing".

Adri didn't take long in the store. She loved everything and couldn't decide, so she decided to get it all! Ginger was going to need it. She also bought a set of luggage with two extra large pieces and asked the clerks to remove the tags off the clothes and fold them into the luggage. Two other clerks appeared from nowhere and before long they were packed up. They must have called the owner. It was a cash sale so that couldn't have been the reason, it must have been the amount of the sale. The owner introduces herself and set down in the sitting area where Adri was sitting. She gave Adri a card and told her, she shipped all over the US and would be glad to have Adri as a customer as Ginger grew up. Adri left, and as she stepped out, Marion was at the door. He opened the door to the limousine for Adri and Ginger then opened the trunk for the suitcases. He was laughing when he got into the car. He said, "You keep surprising me Adri, don't think I've ever met anyone like you." Adri laughingly said, "I hope that is a good thing." Before he could answer, the phone rang. When he hung up, he turned to Adri and said, "That was Cord, he wanted to meet us for lunch." "That sounds wonderful"! Marion drove to the very best five-star restaurant in the city. Adri said, "I'm not sure I've dressed appropriately"? Marion said, "Adri, you look beautiful." She was smiling when she looked up, and Cord was opening the door. Cord took her hand and helped her and Ginger out of the limousine.

Adri didn't realize what a striking couple they were. As they walked in, heads turned to watch the lovely couple carrying a newborn baby. They were seated at a table with a great view of the city. Cord asks Adri if he could hold Ginger. Adri handed her over gently to Cord. Adri said, "Isn't she beautiful. I've seen a lot of babies, and even my own granddaughters were not this beautiful when they were born. They are now, and they also have very sweet personalities. I would love that for her as well". Cord said, "I believe you have fallen in love with my Ginger. I've noticed you carrying her everywhere you go. I only want to say I love it. For the first time in my life, I am being the one that is being taken care of. I've lived a lot of years taking care of everyone around me. I have not only enjoyed it. I feel like I've been taking advantage of you and your hospitality". He pulled a package out of his pocket.

Adri could see it was from the jewelry store. She hoped it wasn't something else for her to return. Cord handed her the gift and said, "A gift for you, for watching after my granddaughters and taking care of me yesterday." Adri opened the package, and the box was beautiful. She opened the box and inside was a gorgeous diamond necklace and exclaimed, "Cord this necklace is beautiful. I love it". She laughingly said, "You know I have spent the morning returning merchandise. I was thinking you had brought me something else to return." Cord wasn't laughing he said, "I'm so sorry about not just the clothes but the whole mess Debbie made that you cleaned up. I have cleaned up Debbie's messes for years. I know how it feels."

The waiter came and took their orders. Adri loved the necklace, she had wanted one like it, but she could never have afforded the size of diamonds that Cord had bought her. She said, "Cord, it was my pleasure. I know we have not known each other long, but I feel close to you, and I have come to love both your Granddaughters. I'm glad we will be spending more time together. Cord said, "I'm afraid I'm going to need you now more than ever." "I need your wisdom to help me with Ginger. I feel like I did my best with Debbie, and I was a total failure. Each time she came back, I would do everything I could think of to surround her with people of quality. If there was a chose to be made, Debbie chose the worst scenario. "The saddest choice of all was her rejection of her children". Adri had tears in her eyes not for Debbie but for Cord.

Their food was served, and it looked delicious. The steak melted in their mouths. Cord loved how the necklace looked on Adri. She looked beautiful. The sparkle from the diamonds and Adri's spark were perfect together. Adri said, "Would you like to tell me more about Debbie"?

Cord began, "Debbie was a cute little girl when I married her mother. I only met her after marrying her mother. She had been staying with her grandmother. I was led to believe it was my wife's mother, but later I learned that it was her father's mother. I'm the one that took primary responsibility for her. Before her mother left, Debbie was dating a boy that was heavy into the drug scene. Debbie and her Mother knew I wouldn't approve. So, Debbie kept her mother's secret, and her mother kept her secret. By the time her mother left, Debbie was just as heavily into the drug scene as her boyfriend. She didn't come home one night, and when I was going to call the police, her mother admitted to me where she was and who she was with. Looking back, I wish I would have called the police, and it might have made a difference. I was still hoping I could get that sweet girl back. Instead, her mother had taught her how to deceive, and her boyfriend had introduced her to some very heavy drugs. When I realized it was out of my control, I hired an agency to kidnap her and place her in rehab. While she was in rehab, she told me about her mother and the name of her mother's lover. I wasn't going to take her word, so I hired a private investigator. He found out more information than I cared to know. There were several men in my wife's life— one who was married. Her married lover's wife was taking him for killing because he had got his wife to keep my wife's name out of the procedure. Before I could confront her, she left and not with the man that had given up his marriage. She went through several disastrous marriages after that she had a serious accident with her current lover and was in a coma before dying after two months".

"Let me back up, I tried to contact Debbie's father after her mother left. Her Grandmother had passed away. My wife had been contacted about her death, but she hadn't told Debbie. Debbie's father was in prison on drug-related charges. It was a sobering picture. I didn't know how to handle Debbie. I took the advice of her counselors in the rehab. We all sat down with her and told her that her mother had filed for divorce. She was also told her mother had moved away and was living with a man named Shores. Debbie threw a fit calling her mother every word in the book. I thought they should let her express her feelings, but her counselors sedated her. When she woke up, she contacted her mother, and her mother checked her out. They didn't even tell me until I went there for my visitation. I had only been allowed to see her every two weeks, and they waited until I came two weeks later to tell me. By that time, I knew she was back with her boyfriend. At least, she had completed her High School education in rehab. I had such hopes for her. The drugs had brought out the worst in her. They told me at the rehab to let her get it out of her system. They said she would come back. She had to find her own way".

Adri was crying now. Cord wrapped her up, and Ginger was squeezed between them. Cord said, "I have never had someone to talk to about Debbie. I don't know why, I know that when I am with you, I feel like there are no barriers. I have hit you with a lot of information, but I want you to have the whole picture. Ginger will have a lot to overcome. If love could overcome, then Debbie would have had a chance. I thought a lot about Debbie and what I could have done differently. I think that I want to be honest with Ginger from a young age about drugs and] their harmful effect. If there ever is a point that Ginger chooses drugs, I seriously don't know if I can follow through, but this time the minute I found out, I would involve the police". Adri said, "It would be hard, but we do what we have to for our children." "It is hard sometimes, but our actions are out of love. Our actions are based on the information we know at the time. That's why you can't grieve over the decisions you made with Debbie. Many girls did take opportunities like you made available for Debbie. Many girls had fewer opportunities than Debbie and still turned their life around". Adri wrapped Cord up and said, "I know whatever decisions you have to make in Ginger's life will be made with unselfish love." They stayed like that for a while.

They set back and ordered dessert. They were in a private area of the restaurant. It seemed very intimate. Cord said, "Adri, you have been there for me starting with you watching over Emmy. I guess what I want to say is I want you to tell me if I ever take advantage of your kindness and generosity. I should be the one to know where that line is, but I have enjoyed you so much. I'm afraid I will lose you or change you in some way". "If there is love at first sight, I have fallen hard for you." Adri said, "Cord, you are easy to love, as well." The two of them kissed for the first time and several more times. When they broke apart, Ginger was awake and smiling. They looked at her and burst out laughing. Cord said, "I have a few days free, and I want us to spend them together." Adri said, "That sounds wonderful"!

When they left the restaurant, Marion was waiting with the door open. They both climbed in, and Cord put Ginger in her car seat. Adri said, "I still have one more stop." When Marion pulled up at the shop, Cord said, "I can do this." Adri said, "No, I've got this down." "Take care of our baby girl." Adri jumped out of the car; Marion had the last two sacks. He walked her up to the shop and opened the shop door and placed the sacks on the counter and walked out the door. Everything went well, and she was back to the limousine quickly. Adri said, "Cord, you can never guess what the total was after I returned all the clothes and accessories."

Cord guessed, "Twenty-seven thousand." Adri said, "No, much higher." Cord guessed, "Eighty-two thousand." Adri said, "Still higher." Cord said, "Higher, One hundred twenty-three". Adri said, "Give up"? Cord said, "Yes, I'm not sure I even want to know now." Adri said, "One hundred seventy-nine thousand dollars." Adri said, "You know I was a teacher/principal, and I never made that much in one year much less had that much go through my hands in one morning." Cord said, "Thanks, Babe, I'll put that in an account for you." Adri said, "No, I have my own money." Cord said, "About that, I can't begin to add up all I owe you for the places you took Emmy and the gifts you bought her. Then yesterday Marion heard you were gifting the two girls that were helping you 50-dollar bills". Cord was smiling, "And we haven't even got to the shopping for Ginger that resulted in 5 suitcases of clothes and other stuff". "You've got a big heart."

Adri said, "I would do it again." Cord said, "You are on my tab from now on. He handed her an American Express card". Adri said, "Wow, I accept." Cord was laughing. Adri said, "Cord, I'm just not into spending crazy money on clothes." "Will I need clothes like that to run with you"? Cord said, "Well, you can use the card if you ever do, but the places we are going for the next few weeks are resorts. You can get away with wearing pretty much anything. The guest is always right". Now they were both laughing. Cord said, "I am usually on a tight schedule." Then he pulled another gift out of his pocket and handed it to Adri. She said, "This is too much." Cord said, "Adri, you are too much. I love everything about you".

Adri stopped and looked Cord in the eyes and said, "I love everything about you." They started kissing, and it became more and more intimate until they realized the limousine had stopped.

They were both smiling, and they looked at Ginger, she was smiling. As they were laughing, Adri held up her gift and finished unwrapping. It was a beautiful gold Rolex with diamond to diamond all over. Adri had never seen anything like it before. She turned it over, and it was engraved. It said, "You're with me." They were both laughing when Marion opened the door. Cord got out, and Adri handed him Ginger, and he offered his other hand to Adri. Adri felt like she was with HIM now.

They went up to the room, and Cord said, "Let me see what all you bought for Ginger today." Adri was happy and surprised that he was interested. She opened the suitcases on one bed and started taking the outfits out one at a time with bows and shoes for all. Cord was impressed. There were several comfortable pajamas, and Cord felt how soft one set was and said, "Let's put this one on her now." Adri said, "Let's bath her first. The biggest sink is in your room." They took Ginger, the new pajamas, and everything they needed. They giggled and laughed through the whole bath, and both of them were wet when they were through. Cord took his shirt off and dried off. Adri then took her top off. She figured she was covered as much as she would have been in her swimsuit. They all got dried, and Ginger got dressed in her pajamas. By the time they finished, they were rolling around laughing on the bed, on Cords bed. When they stopped Cord was on top of Adri and Ginger was asleep on the pillows. Cord and Adri started kissing and touching and getting to know each other's body. They were not even aware that they had now taken their pants off; all that was left was their underwear. They stopped and looked at each other. Cord undid Adri's bra, and she smiled. They began again more slowly and yet more intense. When Cord entered Adri, she said, "Mmm perfect fit. Adri was so tight. Cord nearly came right then. He held back even though every sound of pleasure Adri made was making him come undone. Then he felt her contract and contract again, and he couldn't hold himself back any longer. They were spent. They laid in each other arms for a few minutes then Adri got up and put Ginger in her crib. Cord watched her movements, she hadn't covered herself. He loved her body. She was lovely. Cord felt his life was beginning again.

Adri came back to the bed, and she and Cord made love again before falling asleep. The next morning Cord got up and showered. When Adri heard the shower, she got up and joined Cord. His body was perfection, but no matter what men said about the size. She wanted to tell everyone, it's not the size, it's the fit, and she and Cord were a perfect fit. They put on the luxurious robs the resort provided. There was a knock on the door, and Cord answered it. It was a hotel room service. It looked like Cord had ordered everything that was on the room service breakfast menu. It looked and smelled delicious. Cord had taken care of Ginger when he had first gotten up, so they set down and started enjoying the feast.

When they were finished eating and sitting enjoying their coffee, Adri asked, "When I was cleaning the suite, I never saw any papers about Ginger's birth or hospital stay. Did you apply for her Birth Certificate and her Social Security Card? I wanted to know if the hospital had a photographer, where we could order some pictures of her". Cord said, "I hadn't thought about it again, but I did take a folder the hospital gave me when I checked her out of the hospital. I have just stuck any information that I was given at the hospital in another folder". He got up to get the information. When he came back into the room, Adri said, "Ginger probably has a follow-up appointment. We might want to do that before we leave".

Cord and Adri began going through the papers. Adri found the application for Ginger's Birth Certificate and Social Security Card. She set them aside to fill out later. Cord found a page of thumbnail pictures of Ginger and an order form. He and Adri oohed and awed over how beautiful Ginger was and made up their minds to place an order. Since it was so hard to choose which one, they liked the most, they ordered all of them. They also ordered some collages of pictures framed. Then they continued through the medical records and billing. Adri had finished the stack she was working on and got up to get Ginger. She loved holding her. When she came back into the room, Cord was crying. Adri ran to him, and he was holding a medical report in his hand. Adri wrapped him up in her arms. She was trying to keep Ginger from getting squeezed. Then Adri saw the paper in Cord's hand. She took Ginger back to her crib. Ginger was sleeping soundly.

Adri took the paper from Cord and as soon as she read it, she was on the floor grieving. Cord was now wrapping her up. How long they stayed like that they didn't know. Finally, Cord said, "The bottom of the report gave a time and date of the follow-up report." "It is today." They got back into the shower, but this time they just went through the motions. They seemed undone. Cord was dressed before Adri, and he cleaned and dressed Ginger. Adri was finished about the same time". She said, "She is so beautiful." Then she looked at Cord and said we are the perfect team to get her through this". They walked out together and Marion was there and opened the limousine door. He could see by their faces that something had happened. They were sitting as close as possible for two people. He assumed the problem was nothing between them. They arrived at the hospital. Marion went around the limousine and opened their door. They got out together and proceeded inside, but they continued to the doctor's office trying to stay strong.

Ginger's doctor introduced herself. Her name was Dr. Emily Walters. She said, "She wanted to examine Ginger first. She would also test her again. If her test were still positive, she would speak with them and tell them what they could expect." While she was examining Ginger, she asks several questions. They answered positive to each question, making it very hard to believe that this beautiful little girl could be severely ill. Dr. Walters ask them if they could come back again at 5. She would then have the results of the testing being done on Ginger.

Adri said, "Since we are in the hospital, let's see if we can talk to the photographer"? Cord agreed, "That would be a good idea. Do you mind if I do some research on the internet while you talk with the photographer"? Adri said, "I'm glad you feel able to do that. We need to know what we are facing when we talk to the doctor". "Thank you, Cord for standing strong. I love you so much. I know we can make it through this as long as we are together. Cord, I just can't talk about it yet. Is that OK? Right now, I feel like I am just going to melt down. I am glad I have you. I will do whatever needs to be done for our Ginger. She is so precious".

There was a waiting room right next to the photographer's office. Adri was holding Ginger tight when she walked into the Photographer's Office. She told the girl at the desk that she wanted to place an order and reached in her purse and brought out the paper with the thumbnail pictures. The secretary said she would be happy to help her, and they began going through the pictures and the ideas Adri had. The secretary was very knowledgeable and had great suggestions. They were nearly finished when the photographer came in, and she told the secretary that her appointment had not gone into labor they sent her home. When she spotted Ginger, she said, "I remember you. You should be a week-old today". She turned to Adri and ask, "Did you want to have a photo session today." It only took Adri a moment. She answered, "I would love that. Thank you." The secretary said, "I think we have finished making the decisions. I can finish the forms; you go ahead and take Ginger into the photographer's studio. Adri said, "I would like to get her Papa, I think he would enjoy this." She walked out to the waiting room, and Cord was there leaning his head back with his eyes closed. She knew he was not asleep. Adri said, "Cord, the photographer is here, and she is going to take a few pictures of Ginger. I thought it might be good for both of us. Maybe keep our minds busy".

The photographer was great. She had both Cord and Adri involved and laughing. They had a few moments where they weren't thinking about the news they had learned. Ginger was an adorable baby. The pictures were going to be beautiful! They finished with the photographer and decided to eat in the hospital. They were both quiet at lunch, and neither ate very much. Cord decided to talk to Marion, and he felt Marion needed to know why they were spending the day at the hospital. He also needed to know about Ginger because he had been and would be a part of her life. Adri and Cord were both crying quietly as Cord told Marion.

They left the hospital after the conversation was over. Marion met them at the front door of the Children's Hospital. They were all three silent as they drove back to the motel. When Adri and Cord got back to the suite, Adri changed Ginger into a soft onesie, feed her, and laid her down for a nap. Cord was in bed, and Adri climbed into bed with him. They set the alarm where they could get back to the hospital by 5 pm. It seemed they couldn't hold each other close enough, Cord finally heard Adri's even breathing and knew she was asleep. He later went to sleep, but he didn't know how long he slept. When the alarm went off, they got up and started getting ready to go back to the hospital. Adri changed and dressed Ginger. As always, she looked perfect, but now they were going to see if she was perfect, perfectly healthy.

They arrived on time and were directed straight into Dr. Walters office. Adri wondered if they didn't make you wait if you were getting bad news. She then stopped herself, and she wasn't sure it could be good news. Dr. Walters directed them to sit down. She went around her desk and began speaking, "The lab has tested Ginger's blood and retested, I'm sorry to have to tell you that Ginger does have an active strain. Ginger has been diagnosed with AIDS. We want to start her on medication before you leave today. Our staff will show you how to administer the drugs. There are several, and they have improved the taste. You will be given information about caring for Ginger. It is important that you give her the medication. Her immune system has been compromised, and it would be best for her that she be protected from an environment in which she may catch even the common cold. It could be life-threatening. I want you to know that Ginger's life expectancy is from 1 to 2 years.

Tears were running down Adri and Cord's faces, as they sat stoically listening to Dr. Walters. It was breaking their hearts listening. Dr. Walters finally ended. They left with a stack of information about the medications and also information about AIDS. There was also a schedule of follow up appointments. It was more than overwhelming. It was heartbreaking when they thought about their little Ginger.

They left quietly, and Marion had the car waiting. When they got in the car. Cord told Marion that Ginger had been diagnosed with AIDS. He started to say her life expectancy, but he couldn't finish. Marion said, "I would like to keep Ginger tonight if you would honor my request. I feel you both need to have at least this one evening to yourselves". Cord said, "Thank you, Marion, we are honored at your request and would like for you to keep Ginger for tonight. That would give Adri and I a chance to absorb this information".

When they got to the resort, Marion let them out at the door, and they went directly up to their suite. Adri started getting Ginger things together. She could not stop crying. Cord put the things into the crib and rolled it across the hall to Marion's Suite followed by Adri carrying Ginger. Marion took Ginger, she had been given her dose of medicine for today. Marion said, "I'll wait to hear from you in the morning." They both left crying.

When they got into their suite, Adri went straight to the bed. Cord followed her. He said, "Adri, I have confidence that we can follow this protocol of her medications. I also think we will be able to keep her as safe as far as exposure to other illness. We are both flexible with our schedules, and we can keep her in a safe environment. Adri, I need to know if you are in this with me or not. I understand if you feel that you cannot go through this with Ginger". Adri looked at Cord and said, "Cord, I love Ginger, to leave her now would be as hard or harder than later. If I was to leave her now without doing everything I could for her. I could never live with myself. I love her, and I want to be there for her for whatever she needs for as long as she needs". Adri continued, "I love you! I want to be there with you and for you. We don't know what tomorrow brings for any of us. I have given myself to you, and for me, it is for better or worse. This may be for worst, but I'm staying. You can't get rid of me". Cord said, "I love you. I want you to stay so bad. I didn't know if I could do this alone. I didn't want even to give you a chose, but now I'm glad I did".

They went to sleep and slept soundly. The next morning when Adri woke up, she realized Cord was up and in the shower. She joined him in the shower. Today they were smiling, and today they made love in the shower. They knew that they would both love and protect Ginger as long as they had a chance. They enjoyed a huge breakfast then went across the hall to see Marion and get Ginger. Adri bathed Ginger and fed her with her medicine.

Today they were traveling, Adri put Ginger in her crib before helping Cord pack all the suitcases. They went to the airport; Adri hadn't asked about the flight schedule or tickets. She assumed Cord had it taken care of. When the limousine turned into the gates for the private aircraft, she realized that Cord must have his own plane or have rented one. Marion opened the door for them, and they walked up to the stairs to what appeared to be a new jet. Cord said, "Welcome aboard our jet! Make yourself comfortable. The bedroom is through that door". Adri said, "I have worried all morning how I was going to protect Ginger from being exposed to anything on a commercial flight." "I should have known you had it covered." Cord said, "What else are you worried about"? Adri said, "I just thought maybe we should buy Ginger a mattress." "We could use it in the hotels we stay in. That way, she won't be sleeping on a mattress that someone else has been on before." "I was just thinking how we would get that from city to city, and now it is solved." Cord started laughing, and Adri started laughing.

The flight was very smooth and very comfortable. Adri didn't realize that Marion was the copilot until they landed. Adri and Ginger got into the limousine while Marion and Cord loaded the luggage into the limousine. Then they got into the limousine and headed to the resort. The resort was beautiful. Adri knew without googling that it had a 5-star rating. She was looking forward to the stay. Their suite was gorgeous, and there were loads of amenities. It had every electronic Adri had ever heard of. They had their own concierge. She knew at that moment that Ginger would never have to leave the suite. She set down with

Ginger in her lap and downloaded a few of her favorite authors.

When the valet came up with the luggage, Cord took care of them. He had the new crib put into the master bedroom. Adri was laughing that he had bought a new crib, not just a mattress. He was just as protective as she was. He picked up Ginger and set down by Adri. Adri asks him when his first conference would be. Cord told her, they really just had today. Tomorrow would be his presentation. He asks her if she minded staying in tonight, he needed to look over his notes. She was happy to stay in and enjoy Ginger. They both were happy. Cord ordered their dinner, and it was delicious. Cord told Adri if she wanted to go anywhere or do anything while she was here that Marion would love to watch Ginger. Adri said, "I just downloaded my favorite authors, and I'm set to lay around and hold Ginger and read." "You may get tired of seeing me in my sweats." "This is my kind of vacation." "Thank you for bringing Ginger and me along with you." Cord said, "I'm going to have to thank my granddaughter Emmy for bringing you into my life." "I love you." Adri answered, "I love you, more!"

Adri and Cord had enjoyed their first few days at the resort. Ginger was taking her medicine and eating well. Adri and Cord found time together in bed and the shower. Cord had finished all the technical presentation. The company had bought his product, and now the next few days would be installing the software and teaching the techs the multiple uses. Cord always brought in a team to do this aspect. The team had arrived that morning. Cord had asked Adri if she would like to go out tonight. They decided to eat at a restaurant within the resort, and Marion was coming over to watch over Ginger.

Adri dressed up for the night. When Cord saw her, he was blown away at her beauty. They walked casually over to the Resort Restaurant. They could have gone through the complex, but it was a beautiful night, and they decided to walk outside. It was like walking through paradise. The flowers were beautiful, like a picture of art. Cord was such a gentleman, and Adri loved every minute of the walk. When they arrived, they were treated like celebrities. The service was personalized, and they felt spoiled. The dinner lasted 3 hours, but they hardly knew it, for them the time went quickly.

They walked back in the moonlight but this trip they were less interested in the foliage and more interested in each other. They were indeed a couple madly in love, and anyone watching them could see that. Love was in the air. They went straight for the bed when they arrived back at the suite. They made love again and again.

In the morning Cord and Adri slept in. Cord got up at one point and fed Ginger with her medicine. When he got back to bed, Adri was awake. They made love then ran and hoped into the shower and made love again. They were sitting in the living area. Cord was holding Ginger, and Adri was reading. Cord decided that he was going to go downstairs to Starbucks. He could send the concierge, but he wanted to see what pastry was fresh before he made his decision. He wasn't gone long when his phone rang. Adri saw it was Debbie's numbered. Adri answered, the voice on the phone said. "If you ever want to see Debbie alive than you need to get $100,000 together and I will call back at this time tomorrow with instructions". Adri said, "You might want to call back in about 30 minutes and talk to Cord. I don't care if I ever see Debbie alive. I also need to let you know that Debbie has AIDS. If you have had sex with Debbie, you need to be tested. If you have shared a needle with Debbie, you need to get tested. Debbie has an aggressive strain of AIDS. If you have injured Debbie and come into contact with her blood, you need to get tested. You might keep that in mind. Goodbye". Adri hung up. She wondered what Cord would think about what she had said to the voice on the phone. She felt the call was probably from the creep Debbie ran off with. She thought this person had no idea who Debbie was. Debbie had left clothes worth far more than $100,000 on the floor and thrown around the room. One of the messes Adri cleaned up.

When Cord arrived back at the room, Adri could smell the pastries. Cord said, "What happened? Why are you shaking? Adri said, "It is not Ginger; she is perfect." "Your phone rang, and it was from Debbie's number. I answered it, and the voice on the phone said, "If you ever want to see Debbie alive than you need to get $100,000 together and I will call back at this time tomorrow with instructions". Cord said, "Probably that druggy, she ran off with." Adri said, "You may not be too happy when you hear what I said." Adri continued, "I said he might want to call back in about 30 minutes and talk to Cord. I don't care if I ever see Debbie alive. I also need to let you know that Debbie has AIDS. If you had sex with Debbie, you need to get tested. If you have shared a needle with Debbie, you need to get tested. If you have injured Debbie and come into contact with her blood, you need to get tested. Debbie has an aggressive strain of AIDS? You might keep that in mind. Goodbye". Cord was laughing. It was contagious, Adri started laughing as well. Cord said. "I couldn't have said it better myself. Thank God you were the one who answered the phone" They set down and enjoyed their pastries.

They were through with their pastries when Cord's phone rang. Cord answered. The voice on the end of the line said, "If you ever want to see Debbie alive you need to get $100,000 together, and I will contact you at this time tomorrow to tell you where to drop the cash. Cord said, "Steve, I recognize your voice, and I do not plan on paying you any amount. You wanted Debbie, you got her. I do feel like I should inform you that Debbie does have AIDS. You should be tested". "Don't call back."

Adri was quiet. Cord said, "She is killing my granddaughter." "As far as I'm concerned, she should be behind bars. According to Dr. Walters, Debbie knew before her pregnancy that she had AIDS. She could have used precautions. She has no thought for anyone but herself". "I love Ginger, and I am thankful for every minute we will have with her. I cannot think of the suffering Ginger may go through. I'm praying that she will not suffer". Cord had tears in his eyes, but they were for Ginger, he had no more tears for Debbie.

Marion came over, and the three of them set down at the table. Marion said, "I just got a call from security. They said you just received two calls from Debbie's phone. They said she and Steve are docked in a port near Miami. They wanted to know if you wanted surveillance". Cord said, "The calls were from Steve telling me that if I want to see Debbie alive than I need to get $100,000 together". Marion said, "You realize that the calls were recorded by security." Cord said, "Tell security to turn the tapes over to the Miami Police. If the call comes through again tomorrow, I'll do whatever the police want me to do".

Cord didn't hear anything from the Miami Police. The next day Steve called, Cord answered, and Steve asked if he had the $100,000 together. Cord answered, "Put Debbie on the phone." Debbie came to the phone. Cord said, "Debbie, you know I have the money, what do you need $100,000 for. When you left, you were clear that you never wanted anything to do with me or my money. Now you're calling for $100,000". "I want to know what you want the money for"? Debbie answered, "We got into a little trouble, and it took all our money for bail." Cord said, "What were the charges"? Debbie said, "Pirating." Cord said, "I guess you have a good explanation. Let's hear it". Debbie said, "We were having dinner with another couple on their boat. The old guy just kept bragging about what all he owned and how much he made".

Steve finally had enough and pulled out his gun and told the old man to spread his wealth around. When the old man wouldn't do what Steve said, Steve started shooting the place up. The old guy wet his pants, but he got out the cash and gave it to us". Cord asks, "What did you do"? Debbie said, "Well, when Steve started shooting the place up, I got my gun out and kept it on the wife." "The police said there were other piracy charges as well." Cord asks, "How many"? Debbie said, "Well, it was so damn easy we did a couple more." Cord said, "If you got that money, why do you need money from me"? Debbie said, "Because we bought a supply of drugs, and it took all the money we had. The cops took all the drugs we had so we are flat busted". Then she started laughing at what she had said. Cord was not laughing he said, Debbie, you know you have AIDS right"? She answered, "That's why I need the drugs; they make me forget about all that." Cord said, "Are you taking any of your medication for AIDS"? She said, "No, I don't like the taste."

Cord said. "Well, I need a piece of information from you. Who is Ginger's Dad? You tell me who her Dad is, and I'll have a DNA test run, and if you are telling the truth, then I will check into your case". Debbie said, "I keep telling you I don't know, I was doing a lot of drugs then, and I don't remember everything". Cord said, "Try to remember, and call me back." Debbie said, "We need something now to take the edge off." Cord said, "Try to remember Debbie," and hung up the phone.

Security dialed Cord right after he hung up. He asks them to check into the case and to tell the police what they knew. They will probably be calling us back. The phone rang about an hour later, but it wasn't Debbie or Steve; it was Cord's security. They said the police that was assigned to the case would give us a call. They called us about 10 minutes ago. The charges are attempted murder, murder, piracy on three counts, and intent to distribute. The only reason Debbie and Steve are out on bond is that it was two counts of attempted murder until one of the victims died. It was a child. Cord threw up in the trash can nearest him. Adri could tell whatever was being said was horrible news. Do you have any idea what the police want me to do? They just said if they call again, keep recording.

Cord brought Adri up to speed. He told her they had killed a child. Adri was holding Ginger, and she held her closer. Adri knew how much this must be hurting Cord because he had tried so hard for so many years with Debbie. Adri moved over closer to Cord, and they held each other close waiting to hear from the police or Debbie. The phone rang, and it was Cord's security. They reported that the Miami police had confiscated Steve's boat but that neither Steve nor Debbie was on the boat. They would like us to inform them if we hear from Debbie again. They ask if we felt comfortable making arrangements to hand over cash to Steve and Debbie. If so, they would set up a sting. Cord said that since he had a man in Miami, he would send him to coordinate with the police.

Cord made the necessary calls and then set down close to Adri. Adri had heard the calls. Cord was furnishing two men to coordinate with the police. Debbie would recognize both so that should give her a sense of security. Cord was also furnishing the $100,000 the amount Steve had to ask for. Steve called early. Cord told him to put Debbie on the line. Cord asked, "Debbie, do you have the name of Ginger's Dad"? Debbie said, "I thought about who her Dad could be when I was in rehab before she was born. I was with a group that was snow skiing at the time. I think her daddy is JP Moore, but it could be his younger brother KD Moore". Cord said, "Thank you, Debbie. You will recognize the two security men that I have with the money waiting on your instructions". "I will give you a number that you can reach them and set up a time to meet." Debbie said, "We may need more money because now the police have taken the boat." "We had decided to run because one of the people shot has died." Cord said, "You need to face the charges. How far do you think you can get on $100,000"? Debbie said, "I don't need you lecturing me. We only need to make it to Cuba. Steve has some friends in Cuba that have a place we can stay. They are even going to fix Steve up with a route". Cord said, "A route, what does that mean"? Debbie said, "A drug route." Cord said, "You are going from one bad situation to another, Debbie." Debbie said, "Shut the hell up." "Just give me a number where I can get ahold of your security team." Cord gave her the number and hung up. His security team had been listening, so they knew she would be calling. They also knew Steve and Debbie thought they could make it to Cuba. The security and the police monitored the call when it came through from Debbie and had everything ready for the sting. Debbie had been so spoiled by Cord that she would never expect a double cross. The danger was that Debbie and Steve were both armed.

Cord left to go to the meetings and check on his teams. Mainly they just liked to see him available. Everything seemed to be going smoothly. Everyone was excited about the technology. Cord made a walk through and went back to the suite. He found Adri and Ginger asleep. The stress of the situation with Debbie was exhausting. He laid down with Adri and wrapped himself around her. They both slept. When they awoke, they ordered something to eat.

Cord was taking care of Ginger when he remembered what Debbie had said about Ginger's Dad. Cord called the security and asked them to follow through with what Debbie had said. Cord said, "Coordinate with the attorney concerning the DNA testing." Then Cord hung-up.

The sting was supposed to take place at three that afternoon. Security was supposed to call and report after the conclusion of the sting. Adri and Cord lives were put on hold. Then the phone rang at about 4:30. It was security but not about the sting, it was security calling about the two brothers that Debbie had said could be Ginger's Dad. Security had found out that both brothers lived in San Francisco. They were both gay, and both had partners. When they were contacted, they said they did remember the skiing trips. Debbie was convinced that she could change their sexuality. They traveled with a group of about a dozen. They both had been diagnosed with AIDS, but they were willing to be tested and would love to meet Ginger.

Cord passed on the information to Adri. They both were excited to meet Ginger. JP and KD followed the security instructions about how and where to send their DNA. When the phone rang at 7 pm, it was about the sting. Both Debbie and Steve were in police custody. The police thanked Cord for his cooperation and returned the money to his security team. Cord asked the police if there was any reason he needed to stay in contact with Debbie. They told him no. At that point, Cord stopped answering Debbie's calls.

The DNA results came back that JP Moore, the oldest brother, was Ginger's Dad. Cord had another business conference scheduled. The Moore brothers were anxious to meet Ginger, so Cord and Adri decided that while Cord was out of town on business, Adri and Ginger would fly to California. Marion flew Adri and Ginger to California then flew back home, and he and Cord flew to the business conference.

JP had insisted Adri and Ginger stay with him. A limousine was waiting when they arrived at the airport. Marion drove Adri and Ginger to the home of JP Moore. Marion had planned on staying until Adri and Ginger were settled. Cord had also sent security with Adri that would be staying with them the length of their visit. The minute Adri walked into JP's home, she realized who he and his brother were. They were both renowned artists. How very wonderful for Ginger! Adri had brought each brother an album of photos of Ginger beginning with her birth in the hospital. Both Brothers and their partners were staying at JP's home for Ginger's visit. JP and Doug met Adri and Ginger at the door and welcomed them into their home. They showed Adri, Marion and the security around the home and grounds before Marion left.

Ginger was asleep when they arrived, but Adri could tell that JP was excited to hold her. Adri was thrilled for Ginger, and as soon as they set down to relax, Adri asks JP if he wanted to hold Ginger. He jumped at the opportunity. Doug had hired a photographer that would be staying with them the length of Ginger's stay. JP and Doug brought out pictures of JP when he was a baby.

Ginger looked very much like him. She had the ginger red hair just like both brothers. When it was time to feed Ginger, Adri explained how to mix her medicine with the formula, and as soon as that was done, Adri handed the bottle to JP. He was so moved that he had tears in his eyes as he fed Ginger. He kept saying he had never thought he would have this gift in his lifetime. He and Doug had talked about their desire for children, but the process was very difficult and when he was diagnosed with AIDS. It became impossible. Adri could feel the love between JP and Doug and Ginger. It was magnificent to watch.

KD and Coree arrived around dinner time. Their SUV was full of gifts for Ginger. Ginger was asleep when they arrived, but JP had not put her down. He had been holding her since he fed her earlier. Ginger was beautiful with her Ginger colored hair and her long dark eyelashes. When Ginger woke up, it was as if she knew, and these men were her family. She smiled and held their fingers. All eyes were on her, and she didn't disappoint. Doug fixed her another bottle carefully mixing her formula and medicines as they had been shown and he handed it to JP. It was as if they had been taking care of her forever.

JP finally gave her to his brother to hold. KD was just as moved as JP had been.

After dinner, Adri could see that the four men were comfortable with Ginger, so she said she was going to her room to get some rest. It had been a very exciting but tiring day. She said that if they would like, she would leave Ginger in their care. She had done very little for Ginger all day, but when she offered to leave Ginger with these four men, looked like she was giving the baby a gun to play with. Adri had to laugh. She said, "I'm a very light sleeper. If you need anything just let me know". When she was leaving the room, she heard them teasing each other about taking care of Ginger. Coree wanted a schedule because he still hadn't gotten to hold her yet. Adri went off to her room, laughing.

Adri called Cord the minute she got into her room to tell him how successful the day had been. She told Cord that if she had planned the day herself, she couldn't have asked for more. Ginger was a huge hit, and the four men loved her from the moment they set eyes on her. It made her ashamed for how Debbie had neglected Ginger.

She was crying by the time she finished telling Cord how much Ginger was loved.

The week flew by for Adri. It was like a vacation for her. Ginger had the best of care. When it came time for Adri and Ginger to leave, plans had already been made to return in three weeks. JP and Doug were going to throw a party announcing Ginger. They called it a Sip and See. (Sip Champagne and See the baby) Adri had talked to Cord about the dates during their evening phone calls. He would be doing his last business pitch, but he planned on flying out for the event.

When Adri arrived home, she was happy to be back home. She considered Cord's home her home now. Cord surprised her by coming home a day earlier, and he walked in about an hour after she arrived. He had taken a commercial flight rather than wait on Marion to fly him home. They were both glad to be back together. Adri had already put Ginger to bed when Cord arrived. They had the evening to themselves, and they were happy to take advantage of the privacy.

They slept late, Cord had gotten up earlier and fed Ginger and put her back into her crib. He climbed back in bed, careful not to awake Adri. He knew it had been an emotional week for her. The visit had been centered around Ginger, but as the week went on, Adri observed how weak JP was. She noticed instead of holding Ginger, and he would lay with her on the couch or the bed. The night before Adri left, JP and Doug set with her after supper and told her about JP's battle with AIDS. He had been very sick. The doctors had been honest with him about the amount of time he possibly had. They told him two years if he followed his drug protocol and took care not to contact any illness during that time. JP was now into his third year. He said, 'I'm so glad I didn't give up. Meeting Ginger is more than I ever expected to achieve in this lifetime". "Ginger is truly a dream come true for me."

Adri and Ginger had been home four days when the doorbell rang, and an artist was there with Artwork from both brothers to be hung in Ginger's room. They had to ask Adri about sending art and decor for Ginger's room, and Adri thought Ginger would love it as she got older. The first thing the artist did was set up a computer and FaceTime with JP and KD. They instructed the artist throughout the whole process. When the artist was finished hanging the paintings from both JP and KD, the room was transformed. Adri took Ginger into her room, and it was as if her eyes widened at the completed room. Cord had videoed her with his phone, and he immediately sent the video to JP. JP and Doug called crying after they got the video. It amazed them all the reaction that Ginger had to the art.

Adri and Cord sent pictures and video every day to JP. Quickly it was time for Adri and Ginger to return for the celebration. JP and Doug had planned four clothes changes for Ginger during the celebration. They had also designed the gown that Adri would be wearing. Adri had never had a gown that perfectly suited her more than the gown they designed. It flattered and covered her flaws all at the same time. Cord flew in the day before the Sip and See and joined Adri and Ginger by staying with JP and Doug.

The next day the celebration was to begin at 5:00. As the guest came into the entry between the stair cases leading to the second floor, JP and Doug stood together on one side, and KD and Coree stood together on the other side of a circular gold crib that had a sheer ivory canopy opened in the front to observe the sleeping Ginger haired beauty. Ginger was in an ivory gown of delicate lace. Adri's dress was gold, and she looked beautiful beside Cord in a black tux.

They walked through the event together. There was a string quartet playing in the entry. There was food, drinks, art, and music in every part of the house and lawn. Adri learned later that 542 guests came. The way the celebration had been set up, no one was ever crowded. At 6:00, JP and Doug led the dancing. JP carried Ginger around the celebration as she smiled at everyone as if on cue. It was a perfect night that ended with breakfast at midnight.

Everyone in the household slept in the next day. Miraculously all evidence of the celebration had disappeared except a mound of gifts for Ginger. Ginger, Cord, and Adri stayed two more nights. As they boarded the plane to head back home, Cord said, "It was as if Ginger gave JP life"! Adri said, "You had to see it to believe the difference in him." JP had been thriving at the celebration, but four days later, he was admitted to the hospital. Adri wanted to fly back immediately with Ginger, but JP said it was too dangerous to Ginger's health for her to be around him. He said, "I'm still looking through the thousands of pictures of my beautiful girl." "I have my memories and my love." "Keep my girl safe." Ten days after JP was admitted to the hospital, he passed away. KD was at his side.

At the memorial service, Adri and Cord set on the row behind Doug, KD, Ginger, and Coree. When they came into the service KD was carrying Ginger. She slept through the whole service. The church held 880 mourners. JP was well liked and well known. Doug set stoically during the service. At one point, KD broke down sobbing, Coree took Ginger and handed her to Adri, then Coree wrapped KD in love. Cord, Adri, and Ginger flew back home as soon as the service was over.

A San Francisco Attorney contacted Cord and Adri that JP's entire estate was to be inherited by Ginger. Doug and JP had both agreed to this. Doug was wealthy in his own right and was happy that JP had made this decision. After JP passed away, it was as if KD loss his will to fight any longer. KD passed away two months after his older brother. KD had never gotten healthy enough for Ginger to visit again, but Adri and Cord continued to send pictures and videos. KD did not want a memorial service. He was cremated.

Across the US in Miami, Steve and Debbie's trial dates had been set. They were to be tried separately. Steve was put on trial first. The trial lasted two days, and the jury came back with a guilty verdict on all seventeen counts. The judge sentenced Steve to life in prison without the possibility of parole. Debbie's trial began as Steve's trial was going into the sentencing phase. Against her lawyer's wishes, Debbie took the stand in her own defense. She blamed everyone else, including a dog. (That had been barking). She testified for three days, only making herself look more selfish and self-absorbed. Cord and Adri did not attend the trial. Cord had one of his security people attend and report on the trial to him. Cord picked someone Debbie did not know because he did not want her to be aware of his interest. Debbie was found guilty on all seventeen counts and sentenced to life without the possibility of parole.

Forty-eight hours after Steve and Debbie were sentenced, they were placed in separate Florida Prisons in cell blokes with other prisoners that were sentenced to life without the possibility of parole. Within 24 hours of that placement, both Steve and Debbie had bccn stabbed to death. The coroner's report said that they had been stabbed 17 times with the 17th time as the fatal blow.

Cord and Adri were back at home. Ginger was gaining weight but only an ounce or two at a time. She didn't appear to be in any pain. She could now lift her head. Cord and Adri objective with Ginger at this point was to keep her eating and on her medicine regiment. They enjoyed her little smiles, and they were very protective that she was not exposed to anything that may make her sick. They kept her at home the majority of the time unless they were traveling together. The whole staff was protective of her. If anyone had the least cold, they stayed away from her.

When Ginger was five months old, Adri woke with a migraine headache. Adri woke up, throwing up. She threw up in the bed and on the floor of the bathroom before she could make it to the toilet. Waking with a migraine was the worst because she was already sick with the pain and you couldn't keep any medication down. Adri picked up Ginger and made it downstairs to find Cord. Cord was in his office on the phone. Adri walked into the office just as he was hanging up. Whatever the phone call was about Adri could tell Cord was upset. Adri asked, "Cord, can you watch Ginger. I have woken up with a migraine". Cord said sharply, "Sorry, I have two more calls, and a conference call at 9 am". "This is what you paid to take care of." Adri couldn't believe he said that. She said, "Show me the money." As she walked out of the room. She threw up again before she made it to the bathroom. Sheila and Missy were cleaning the room. Adri apologized for being sick and making such a mess. They told her the bed was ready for her whenever she was ready. She thanked them and went into the bathroom and ran a bath. She undressed herself and Ginger and fixed Ginger a bottle with her medicine. She was still having problems with her vision and the feeling in her right hand. She was careful not to hold Ginger too tight. When she got the bottle ready, she put it on the side of the tub and climbed in with Ginger. She fed Ginger as she soaked in the tub. She had wrapped Ginger in a hand towel where she wouldn't get chilled. After Ginger was fed, she burped her and then rinsed her and laid her on her shoulder. Adri closed her eyes, but the pain was so bad she couldn't get comfortable. Cord realized what he had said to Adri, and he felt terrible. He was so upset about the call, and he had taken it out on Adri. What he said hadn't even made sense because he and Adri had never discussed money and he knew Adri used her own money paying for things and services for Ginger. He had been very generous with her when they first met, but he never had reimbursed her for her generosity. They seemed to be wrapped up with Ginger, and her parent's situations and the discussion of money had just not happened. He was a very wealthy man, and he had no excuse for not taking care of Adri. Cord walked upstairs to apologize to Adri. Sheila told him Adri was in the bathroom bathing Ginger. When he walked in, Adri was laying in the tub, holding Ginger. They both had their eyes shut. Cord stopped and stared at Adri. She was so beautiful. He wished he had a picture of her and Ginger just like they lay. Tears came to his eyes. He turned and left the bathroom.

Adri asked Sheila to please have Marion bring the limo around to the front for her. She dried

Ginger and put a soft pink warm-up suit on her. Then she dried herself and put on her favorite soft pink warm-up suit. She checked the diaper bag, put her billfold in it, and walked down the steps and out the door. Marion was waiting for her, and she asks him to put Ginger in her car seat. She explained, she was having a migraine and was still having trouble with her vision and her pressure with her grip. She asks Marion to take her to the nearest emergency room. They arrived within a few minutes. Marion opened the door and took Ginger out of the car seat, then he walked around and opened the door for Adri. Adri asks if he would bring in the car seat for her. Marion helped Adri, and they were finally at the check-in desk.

Adri explained that she had woken up with a migraine and that she had been throwing up ever since she woke up. Those were the magic words. They took her to an exam room, and the nurse hooked her up to an IV for nausea. Adri was having trouble holding Ginger, so she turned two chairs around and lifted the car seat upon the chairs and used her seat belt. Ginger had not rolled over yet, but Adri was taking every precaution. The nurse took Adri's vitals, and her blood pressure was high, probably due to the pain.

The nurse asked if Adri had anyone that could watch the baby, and Adri told her she didn't. The nurse said that they could not give her anything for the pain unless there were someone else to watch the baby. Adri asked if the hospital had a daycare, she would be willing to pay someone to watch Ginger. It was at that moment that the nurse's daughter came to the door to wave her Mom goodbye. Adri said, "Wait!" "Can she possibly watch Ginger until I am released." The girl, Shelby, said, "Please, Mom, I want that Prom Dress." Shelby looked at Adri when her mom hesitated and said, "I have baby set my neighbor since he was a month old. He is now two. I have taken the babysitting classes offered by the Dept. of Human Services. I would love to watch Ginger if you want me to". Adri said, "I would love for you to watch her." You can take her out of the carrier and hold her if you like. She has already eaten. She will probably sleep a couple of hours". "Thank you so much"!

Adri laid down on the examining table and closed her eyes. The doctor came in and wrote the orders for the oxygen and a shot for the pain. When Adri was finally getting some relief, she asked Shelby, "How much is the Prom Dress you want"? Shelby said, "It is $275, which is more than I have ever spent on a dress for anything". Adri said, "Can you hand me my billfold out of the diaper bag"? Shelby held Ginger close and got the billfold. Adri said, "I would like to buy your Prom Dress." She handed Shelby $300 then she said, "You'll need shoes" and gave her another $100 and "You'll need to buy a picture for your Mom." "Even if you never go out with the guy again, it's always fun to look back at what you wore and how your hair was fixed." "Oh yeah, You'll need hair and nails" and handed Shelby another $100. Shelby was so excited, and she twirled around with Ginger. Adri said, "I had a real emergency, and you helped me out, now I want to help you out." Shelby started crying. She said, "My mom and I are on our own. My Dad left her for his secretary. He is supposed to pay child support, but he never does. I never dreamed I would be able to get this dress. Thank you. Thank you. Thank you." Adri was so touched. Adri said, "I'll talk to your Mom and let her know it was what I wanted to do." Then Adri felt asleep.

The nurse woke Adri up and said your ride is here. Adri looked up, and Cord was at the door. He walked straight to the bed and told Adri, "I'm so sorry, I promise I will never talk to you like that again. Everything I said was a lie. Please forgive me. I do want to talk to you about it when you are feeling better, but for now, I want you to know that I am not that person. I'm so sorry". Adri said, "OK." Then Cord said, "Where is Ginger"? He hadn't notice Shelby holding Ginger, and he had been so focused on Adri. Adri said, "Cord, can you wait outside." Cord looked so sad, but he stepped outside the door.

Adri said to the nurse, "I have given your daughter money for her Prom Dress, Shoes, Pictures, Hair, and nails. I hope that covers everything. I was happy to do it for her. She saved me from my emergency, but I just like her and her attitude. She was ready to step up and work for her dress, and I admire that". Now the nurse and Shelby were both crying. Adri said, "I can also get the appropriate agency to collect your back-child support. Plus get your husband set up where his support goes through the agency. I want to help you out if you could give me his name and information". The nurse said, "Thank you! It looks like we all met today for a reason, and each of us helped the other out of an emergency". They all hugged and said, "Thank you." Then

Adri took Ginger and opened the door. She asked Cord to get Ginger's car seat, and Adri and Cord walked together to the limousine.

When they got home, Cord said, "You go get in bed." "I'll take care of Ginger." Adri walked straight up to the Master Bedroom and climbed into bed. She didn't wake until the next morning. When she woke up, Cord was right there and asked her if she thought she could eat anything. She nodded her head yes and headed to the bathroom. When she came out of the bathroom Cord had a huge breakfast waiting on a table in front of the windows. The food tasted delicious. Cord said, "Babe, I love you. I'm so sorry I acted like I did yesterday morning. I owe so much to you, and I'm not talking about money. You are the first and only person that I have ever had in my life that wasn't using me for my money. I'm so sorry. Can you forgive me"? Cord was crying. He said again, "I love you." I don't ever want to make you feel like I don't appreciate you". Adri said, "Cord, you don't need to explain. I knew you were mad about the call, and I knew what you said to me was what you wanted to yell at the person on the other end of the phone. You were right, I could take care of Ginger on my own, and I did".

"I love you"! "Our relationship is not that fragile." "Well, I hope it isn't." Cord wrapped Adri in his arms and said, "I need to know you forgive me and you know I'm truly sorry," "I went upstairs to tell you how sorry I was, and you were in the bath. I didn't want to disturb you. Then when I went up to check on you again, you were gone. It broke my heart, and I thought I had lost you". Adri said, "I forgive you. I know you are truly sorry."

Cord asks, "Adri, do you feel like going out tonight. Maybe somewhere nice to eat". Adri said, "That sounds wonderful, I'm always hungry for red meat after a migraine." "Maybe somewhere that has great steak." Cord said, "I'll make the reservations." Adri laid back down and took a nap. She made sure to set her alarm before she went to sleep. She was really surprised when the alarm woke her up. She had plenty of time to get ready, but before she got in the shower, she walked over to Ginger's crib to check on her. She was not in the crib, so Adri assumed Cord was watching her.

Adri got in the shower and enjoyed the hot water. She felt wide awake and knew from migraines in the past that it was over, and she would be able to enjoy the evening. She picked a lacy dress that was very flattering. She had taken a cue from JP and Doug and now knew what styles flattered her figure the most. Cord came up to get ready, and Adri saw Ginger was already dressed. She checked the diaper bag, and it was also ready to go. Adri finished dressing and went downstairs with Ginger. Everyone was very complimentary. She again apologized about being sick yesterday. They were very kind about it. She told them that she usually wasn't sick when she had migraines because as soon as she felt one coming on, she took medicine for nausea. It was only when she woke up with a migraine that it was too late to keep any medicine down. They said, again and again, and you don't need to apologize.

When Cord came downstairs, he looked very handsome in black on black. He stopped on the stairs and took a second to enjoy looking at Adri, she was gorgeous, and holding Ginger made her even more desirable. He complimented Adri on her beauty and handed her roses. Adri thanked Cord and complimented him on how handsome he looked. She had tears in her eyes because no one had ever given her roses before. They walked out the door hand and hand. Marion was standing by the limousine and opened the door for them. Adri got in with Ginger and Cord, and Marion went around to the other side of the limousine to get in. Adri put Ginger into her car seat, which was in the seat facing them. Ginger still rode facing backward, which in the limousine meant she was facing them.

Adri hadn't asked where they were going after their conversation this morning. There were so many nice places, and she knew she would be happy with Cord's choice. Then they pulled up to the building that had a revolving restaurant on the top. It was called "Top Of The World. She looked at Cord and said, "Perfect." He smiled at her. Cord reached into Ginger's car seat and released Ginger while Marion opened the door for Adri to stepped out. Cord was carrying Ginger and Adri was carrying her roses. She loved the smell. They were directed to the elevator. Cord put his free arm around Adri, and she lends into him. They were greeted and shown to their table as soon as they stepped off the elevator. They were seated at the window with their seats side by side, looking out the window at the view of the city. Cord had ordered for them, and they were served immediately. Adri loved coke and Cord loved sweet tea. Their firsts course was a shrimp cocktail followed by a salad with everything that Adri loved in the salad. Adri was thinking Cord was so thoughtful. Then came the T-bone steak with a huge loaded bake potato. Adri noticed the sun was setting. She took Cord's hand, and they enjoyed watching the sun go down over the city.

For the next couple of months, Adri and Ginger traveled with Cord. They would see the sites in the cities wherever they traveled. Adri and Ginger would take group tours during the day while Cord was busy with work. Adri was very careful to keep Ginger covered with light chiffon material. Adri was also very careful to keep Ginger to the side or back of any group. Cord's travel was always, without exception scheduled around Ginger's appointments.

When Ginger started lifting her head, the doctor had ordered physical therapy for Ginger. All the therapy was taught to Adri, and she carried out the exercises with Ginger at home. Adri was shown the range of motion exercises and other exercises to carry out through play to stimulate Ginger to roll over and start sitting up. The doctor wanted Ginger to try to stay within her developmental range in every area, even if she was small. Ginger was holding her head up, reaching for toys, and also rolling over now. The doctor explained that they were not worried about introducing Ginger to foods, she was getting a super dose of nourishment in her various formulas and was still gaining weight but still only an ounce at a time. Adri and Ginger were now spending a lot of time doing play therapy. Adri would be in the middle of an activity and Ginger would be responding when they would have to stop to mix the formulas and the medicines which were now varying because they were monitoring Ginger's blood and making changes accordingly.

After Ginger's last appointment, Cord had suggested to Adri that they might consider hiring a nutritionist. Ginger's formula now needed to be measured and mixed. Her diet, as well as her medications, were changing with her needs, sometimes weekly—many ingredients needed to be ordered and ready when Ginger needed. Ginger's diet and medications were becoming very time-consuming. The cost of a nutritionist was not an issue because of the money Ginger's Dad had made sure was easily accessible for her.

The only problem was finding a nutritionist that would not mind traveling.

The third day Adri set interviewing men and women for the position she was getting discouraged. Then her second appointment walked into the study. Her name was Linda. After the introduction was made, the applicant asked to meet Ginger. This was the first applicant that had ask to meet Ginger, and Adri was thrilled. Adri could tell immediately that Ginger had stolen Linda's heart! This was exactly the relationship Adri was looking for them to have. Ginger's diet and medications would always be a part of her life, and Adri wanted a nutritionist who would love and motivate Ginger. Adri did not want this aspect of Ginger's life to turn into some power struggle that would ultimately upset Ginger.

When Adri ask Linda if she would be able to travel with the family, Linda answered that she would look forward to traveling. She said that her husband had passed away two years ago, and because they did not have any children, she had a flexible schedule. Adri was so impressed that she took Linda a tour of the staff's apartments. The apartments were furnished with modern furniture.

Adri could tell that Linda was impressed with the size and furnishings. The way the house was designed, each apartment had an outside entrance and courtyard.

They had just finished touring Ginger's Suite. The suite included Ginger's bedroom and bath, and also an adjacent bedroom and bathroom for Linda's use, in case Linda might need to stay close and monitor Ginger, and a full kitchen and seating area. Linda was impressed with the thought that had gone into making everything convenient for the care giver. They were coming back downstairs when Cord and Marion came in the front door. Everyone was ready for lunch, so the four of them went into the kitchen nook and enjoyed the buffet that had been set out for lunch. Cord took Ginger from Linda, and he held her while he was eating like it was something he often did, which it was. Ginger was still on a schedule of eating every two hours, but Adri had fed her prior to Linda's appointment, and it was still another hour until her next feeding.

Everyone enjoyed the conversation, and Adri could see Cord and Marion were as impressed with Linda as she was. Ginger and the three of them were the nucleus of the traveling family, so Adri was very happy Linda fit in so well.

After lunch, Adri took Ginger to feed her while Cord and Linda went to the library. Cord discuss the salary and benefits with Linda and offered her the job as Ginger's nutritionist. Linda was very pleased with the package, and it was nearly twice what she was making now. Cord also discussed with her the budget which she would need for her position. The bottom line was pretty much, whatever Ginger needed to feel free to purchase!

The next three days, Linda settled into her apartment and her routine. She had Gingers formula ready every two hours, and her medications were ordered, Linda had those available as well. Adri loved it and never failed to tell Linda how much she appreciated her and the extra time it allowed her to spend with Ginger.

Cord announced to both Linda and Adri that they would be flying to San Francisco the next morning. Linda was excited, but a bit nervous. The first thing she did was pack plenty of formula and all Ginger's medication. Then since Marion's apartment was closest to her, she knocked on his door. When Marion answered, she told him she was packing and ask if he could advise her. He said to her that other than her responsibilities to Ginger, she would be free to tour and explore San Francisco as she liked. Linda thanked him and went back to her apartment to start packing. She thought, what was I thinking about asking a man what to pack. Of course, his apartment had been the most convenient, but she decided she probably needed to talk to Adri.

Linda walked down the hall to the main kitchen and found Adri and Ginger. Adri was having coffee and offered Linda a cup. Linda accepted and set down with Adri to visit about what she should pack. Adri was very excited. She told Linda that she had gone online looking for day tours of San Francisco and the surrounding area. Adri showed Linda the day tour for San Francisco and invited Linda to go with her. Linda was very excited, but before she accepted, she offered to keep Ginger while Adri took the Day Tour. Adri immediately said that she always took Ginger with her. Adri went on to say that if at any time Ginger's health became an issue, she would call Marion to pick them up. Adri went on to say that she had only called Marion once and that was because there was another woman with children on one of the trips and the women and her children kept getting in Gingers face and touching Ginger. No matter what she said to them, Adri was unable to protect Ginger. She had called Marion and left the tour. Linda knew that Adri was very protective of Ginger's health.

Adri also told Linda she had found one tour where they would take the ferry to Sausalito and have lunch and shop. They decided to book both tours. Adri suggested packing comfortable clothes and a couple of pairs of walking shoes for the trips. She also suggested Linda pack a nice dress or two because the four of them would probably go out some evenings for nice dinners. She and Cord enjoyed trying the cuisine of the areas they visited.

Linda was excited beyond belief. This was a dream come true for her. She packed everything Adri had told her. She also put in a black outfit for daytime and black dress for the evening and added several colorful scarves. That way if she needed, she could wear the clothes twice and changeup with scarves. She was packed and ready to go with her luggage, and the luggage for Gingers formula and meals in the hall outside her apartment door like Marion had instructed her earlier. She went down the corridor with her purse and a small soft-sided cooler that had what Ginger needed for the next few hours.

She knew she was early, but when she arrived in the kitchen. Cord, Adri, Ginger, and Marion were all there to greet her. As they went out the front door, Linda saw security putting her bags in the Limousine trunk. Marion asks Linda if she would like to sit up front with him, and she didn't hesitate to say yes. Marion made driving in rush hour traffic seems easy. Soon they arrived at the airport and drove over to the terminal designated for the private airplanes. Marion drove right up to a jet on the tarmac, and everyone started getting out. Marion told Linda to go ahead and go up the stairs, and her luggage would be unloaded by the crew.

Linda followed Adri, carrying Ginger up the stairs. Adri gave her a quick tour. During the tour, she showed her the kitchenette but asked her to put Gingers formula and medicines in the refrigerator in the bedroom. Linda marveled at the jet's luxury, and she also recognized that someone had put a lot of thought and planning into the accommodation that Ginger would need.

When the outer door was shut, Adri and Ginger took a window seat, and Cord took the aisle seat next to them. Marion directed Linda to the window seat across from them, and he took the aisle seat by Linda. Cord and Marion had a low conversation across the aisle, Linda could hear enough to know that it was about the flight route and pilots.

Marion turned to Linda and asked her if she had flown before in a small jet. Linda told him she had only flown commercial and not really that much. Marion assured her that she was in the best of hand. He went on to tell her that there were two pilots in the cockpit. They had both flown for several years for Cord. Also, he and Cord were both pilots with instrument ratings, so there were four pilots on board. He continued to talk to Linda because she did appear anxious. He told her that Cord kept his planes in tip-top condition. If there was a question about parts, he replaced with new. His mechanics loved him because he always followed their suggestions.

Adri noticed that Linda and Marion seemed to be in serious conversation as soon as the plane reached its flying altitude and leveled out. Adri, Ginger, and Cord got out of their seat belts and walked back to the living quarters of the plane. Marion got out of his seat belt and moved to a seat across from Linda and facing her. He brought a table up out of the wall. He showed Linda where all the electronics were stored. There were laptops, iPads, even the latest iPhones. He told her she was welcome to use any of them. Then he asks if Linda played cards, she told Marion that she loved to play cards and that she had to warn him, she was very competitive. They talked about different card games and decided on poker. During the game, Linda told Marion that she also played electronic games. She said she had never gone online and played against strangers, she had only played against friends she knew. They both decided that they would love to play against each other the first opportunity they would have on the trip.

A stewardess offered them salads, sandwiches, and snacks throughout the trip. When they were finally back to even with their scores, they decided to stop and have a sandwich. They talk about gaming the whole time they were eating. Linda could not believe her luck, she had found the ideal job and was getting to use her educational background, she was getting to travel and enjoy the sights and on top of everything she had found a competitive gamer! She couldn't be happier.

When the plane got into the pattern for landing, Adri, Ginger, and Cord came back to their seats. When Marion saw them, he told Linda this would have to be their last hand. For a while, he added. Marion put the table up and set back down by Linda, and they fastened their seat belts.

Adri and Cord both noticed the difference in Marion and Linda. They were talking and teasing and laughing. They were totally consumed with each other. It was really fun for Adri and Cord to watch.

The plane landed, and everyone started moving at once. Linda picked up her purse and went back to the living quarters and loaded the small soft-sided cooler with the formula and medicine that had not been used. She was the last to leave the airplane. As she came down the stairs, Marion met her and told her to go ahead and get in the limousine, and her luggage would be taken care of.

She got into the front seat and after everything was loaded Cord got into the back with Adri and Ginger and Marion got in the driver's seat.

Linda was overwhelmed when they pulled up to what she knew must be a 5 Star Resort. Every direction she turned was picture perfect. She was thinking if this is all I see of San Francisco I'll be a happy traveler! They were shown to a suite of rooms. There was a general living area with a full kitchen, then to one side was a suite of 3 rooms that were arranged with a Master Suite and luxurious spa bath and two smaller rooms adjoining. All three rooms had spacious balconies with great views of the city and harbor. By the Master bed, there was a new pink bassinet, especially ordered and delivered for Ginger and beside the bassinet was a diaper table fully stocked. Then in one of the adjoining rooms, there was a new Baby Crib and diaper table set up fully stocked. There was a stack of new crib sheets. The primary colors of the room were different shades of pink and green. There was also a new area rug with play areas set up and a toy box that was overflowing. Adri told

Linda that hotel rooms were full of germs. She said that Cord paid for a cleaning team to prepare their room when they traveled. She said I contact a decorated and she prepares the room for Ginger. When we leave, we donate the items to a home for unwed mothers in the area.

Adri said, "It may seem a little over the top, but we want Ginger to be happy and safe, so we do everything we can think to do to make that happen." Linda said, "I'm so impressed with Ginger's care." "God gave you a special gift when he placed Ginger in the care of you and Cord." "You both were God chosen for her." Adri and Linda hugged, and Adri knew she had found a kindred spirit.

The concierge continued the tour by taking Marion and Linda through the Living Area to two suites that adjoined the living area. They were identical, king size bed in a large bedroom with a balcony with a beautiful view of the city and harbor. They also each had a spacious spa bath built for two. Before Linda could contain herself, she said, "I can't wait." She realized what she said when she heard Marion say, "I can't either." They both stopped and looked at each other. Then he took her hand, and they left the bath laughing.

Marion told Linda that after traveling, Adri and Cord usually order room service. He said Cord spends the evening going over his presentations and Adri and Ginger adjust to their new home. Linda asks Marion if he would like to order room service and eat out on the balcony. He told her he would love that.

The luggage arrived, and everyone went to their rooms to unpack. Linda put all her things away then she rolled Ginger's suitcases to the kitchen. She had taken up a whole kitchen cabinet by the time she was finished unpacking and organizing. It was 10 minutes until Gingers next feeding. Linda took the ice chest, which had one more feeding in it. She walked over to Adri and Cord's Suite and knocked on the door. Adri answered in cute pajamas. Linda apologized for disturbing her, but Adri quickly explained that she always relaxed in her PJ's. She said She loved the feel of the soft fabric. Linda handed her Ginger's next feeding/meds and Adri said for Linda to fix Ginger's feedings/meds for the night and leave them in the main kitchen refrigerator.

Adri also said that there were a mini fridge and bottle warmer in the Master Suite. She said she would get them when Ginger needed them.

Adri said, "Don't forget our City Tour tomorrow!! Do you want to meet for breakfast before the bus picks us up?" Linda agreed, and they decided to meet to go to breakfast at 9 in the morning.

Linda went back to the main kitchen and fixed Ginger's formula and her medications for the night. She lined them up and labeled them with the times because the formulas and medications varied.

Then Linda went to her room, twisted her hair up, and stepped into the luxurious spa bath. The warm water and air jets felt wonderful. She had used the products supplied by the resort, they had a pleasant smell, but best of all, was how silky her skin felt. She closed her eyes for a few minutes. There was a knock on the door. She yelled I'll be right there. She could tell it was the door adjoining Marion's suite. She was thinking, 'How long did I sleep' when she saw the bedroom clock and realized it had been an hour. She threw the Resort Bathrobe around her and opened the door. Marion was stunned silent. She was the most beautiful women he could ever remember seeing. Matter of fact he couldn't even think of another woman. Her hair was clipped up, her cheeks were flushed, and her breast was flushed, he could see most of her breast because of the way she had hurriedly wrapped the bathrobe. Plus, she was wet, and the robe clung to her figure in a very provocative way.

Finally, Linda spoke first. She told him she had fallen asleep in the spa bath and lost track of time. This image just made his jeans tighten. Thank goodness he had decided on jeans instead of his linen shorts. She saw the menu and turned to get it and what caught his attention was her wet robe clinging to her back and bottom. She turned and handed him the menu and ask him if he minded ordering while she got dressed. She added as she walked toward the bedroom, for him to just order her whatever he ordered. Then she was gone.

He stood stunned, and he had been so glad that they were getting along so well because he knew they would be spending a lot of time together, especially when Cord traveled. He was really surprised that he was feeling so attracted to her. He had not even dated since his divorce. He had thought he would never open his life much less his heart to another woman again. He couldn't think of anything but how she looked in her bathrobe!!

He realized he was holding the menu! He could not think straight. He finally ordered their house special for two, and he was proud of himself that he remembered to say they wanted it set up on the balcony.

There was a knock on the door, and Marion answered it. It was the concierge, Marion recognized him. He directed the bell boys with him, and 3 minutes later, the patio was transformed. There was a table and two dining chairs. The table was covered with a tablecloth, and the straight back linen chairs had red satin bows tied around them. The lounging furniture and table had been set up to the side where they could still be used if anyone wanted.

The centerpiece for the dinner table was brought in, and it must have been two dozen red roses. The bell boy took them out of the vase, Marion saw the roses were in a tube of water. The bell boy wrapped the rose stems again and again with wide red silk ribbon and finished it off by tying a beautiful bow. The arrangement was beautiful enough for a bride to carry. It was at that moment that Linda appeared. She was in a lovely silk dress with broad art strokes on a background of red. It was a maxi dress, but because of the slit, Marion was able to enjoy her long legs that he glimpsed with every step. He said, "You look beautiful, Linda." She blushed, and he knew he was falling hard for her. Linda said, "Thank you, Marion." "I'm embarrassed that I fell asleep." Marion said, "Come see the patio. They have transformed it." He took Linda's hand, and they walked across the living area to the patio. Linda said, "Thank you, Marion. I love it."

The concierge handed them each a glass of champagne, then left the bottle on the table in a unique holder. They both tasted the champagne. Linda asks Marion what he decided to order them. He told her he had ordered the Resort special for two. Linda said, "I think I'm going to like being a party of 2". The concierge asks if they were ready for their shrimp cocktails. Marion pulled out a chair for Linda, and she set down, and he took the chair opposite. Their shrimp cocktails were served, then Shrimp Louie Salads were served, as their last bites were taken, their dishes were quietly removed, and the next course appeared which was Grilled shrimp, Grilled Vegetables, with a Steak. As they were eating, Marion had been pointing out the sights in the City and Harbor. Linda was so excited, some of the places he was telling her about had been listed on the Travel Tour they were taking the next day.

The concierge brought their Triple Chocolate Cake covered with Fresh Strawberries. He said he would be leaving them alone now but if they needed his call and him left a number. They both thanked him and told him everything had been wonderful. They finished their dessert and coffee. Marion took Linda's hand, and they stood at the rail watching the city come alive in the night. Linda said, "I love being a party of two." Marion leaned over and kissed her. Linda stepped into the kiss. Both of them were caught up in the kiss when they stopped, and they stood looking at each other. Linda said, "I don't know where this is taking us, but I'm enjoying spending time with you." "I think I better say good night." Marion kissed her again and said good night.

Linda set her alarm and got in bed. 'Was she crazy.' Had she only known Marion a week? Maybe he seduced all the women in the household? It sure would be convenient? But then again, he was respected by Cord and Adri, and she trusted their judgment? He was very accomplished, and he had traveled a lot? Oh, she was very confused but mostly about her feelings. She hadn't even dated since her husband had passed away. Oh, she had been pursued, and some had tried to put their arms around her; some also tried to kiss her. She had been completely turned off and found it hard even to be civil to get away from them. She really thought she would never be interested in another man and here she was falling fast for the gentleman was a good kisser,

Linda awoke with the alarm. She threw on the Resort robe and went to the kitchen. The first thing she did was start the coffee. Then she started fixing everything Ginger would need for the day. Marion came in dressing for the day, and she felt like a bum still in the robe. She had no idea his reaction to her wearing that robe.

He filled her cup back up and got himself a cup. Then he saw her flushed cheeks, and he couldn't resist, he kissed her. She told him that she and Adri and Ginger were going on the sightseeing tour. She finished packing Gingers formula/medicines in the soft sided ice chest. He told her he and Cord would be at the resort all day. They would make sure everything was set up to kick off the presentations the next day. He said Cord was a perfectionist. They would check the sound systems, the technology, the seating, even the menus for the conference. It would be a busy day. Linda said she had to get ready. She was meeting Adri for breakfast. Marion kissed her before she left. It was very domestic. She couldn't believe she was thinking that. Linda wore a short shirtdress and walking sandals. Adri had on a T-shirt dress and walking sandals. They met in the living area and headed down to breakfast. Adri had brought a stroller, so Linda put the small cooler in the bottom shelf of the stroller. Cord called Adri and said there was a buffet, but it had a line so he and Marion had got a table for 4 when it was their turn so if they wanted to join them, they wouldn't have to stand in line. Adri said that was an offer she couldn't refuse.

When the elevator opened, they saw Cord and Marion right away. They had ordered the girls coffee and the buffet. Adri and Linda both said, "Good job." At the same time and they all headed for the buffet laughing. Cord carried Ginger. Marion was right behind Linda. He told her quietly how beautiful she looked. It made her blush. When he saw her blush, he said I love to see you blush. Maybe tonight I'll tell you why. Linda said, "Your pretty handsome today yourself." She actually thought he blushed. Then she leaned in and said, "You're also a really good kisser."

They filled their plates and went back to the table. Everyone was talking about their day. Before they realized it had been an hour and over the sound system, an announcement came that the tour bus had arrived. The guys got up with the girls, and while Cord was busy with Adri and Ginger, Marion put his arm around Linda and kissed her on the cheek. She walked off laughing.

Adri was so glad to have Linda with her. The hardest part of taking Ginger in public was protecting her, because of her immune system. Together they made a natural barrier, and people didn't get in Ginger's face or touch her. They talked and took pictures. They couldn't have picked a better tour. They had fun running around getting pictures of everything. Ginger was perfect. She smiled and giggled with them. She wasn't having any trouble with her formulas or medication. This was her life, and Linda prayed she would always be this cooperative.

When they got back to the resort, they were exhausted. The guys were in the suites waiting for them. Someone in the sound crew today told them about a pizza place that was within walking distance, and they had thought it would be a good place to go tonight. Everyone agreed. Linda said she needed a minute to mix Ginger's formula and get her medicines. She went to the kitchen, and Marion followed. Marion asks if he could help, and Linda explained her system. She really didn't know how late they might be so she made the next two feedings. Marion said, "I told Cord that I was enjoying spending time with you." Linda turned around and looked at Marion, waiting. Finally, she could wait no longer, and she said, "What did he say"? Cord told me that it was about time I started dating again, and he thought I had chosen well. They could hardly kiss for their big smiles.

They walked back into the living area, and Cord was coming in from the bedroom. He had changed Ginger, and she was in a soft, comfy, and very cute outfit. They went out the side of the hotel to avoid the front desk area. The company employees that would be in the workshop would be checking in all evening and Cord did not want to interact until tomorrow. He had a routine that worked for him, and he stuck with it.

The pizza place was an experience itself. There were live entertainers on stage, and they changed every 20 minutes unless the audience calls them back for an encore. The tables were close together, and the place was full. They happened to get a great table, and Marion was glad the tables were close, he kept his leg pressed up against Linda's the whole night. He could tell by her blush that it was affecting her. They put baby ear plugs in Ginger's ears and then put a little bonnet on her head that hid them. She slept through the whole evening. Cord and Adri talked in each other's ears, and Marion and Linda did the same. There was no way to talk over the table; it was so noisy. They were all enjoying the pizza and entertainers. Marion put his arm around Linda, and he would hold her hand. They seemed to be touching all evening when Cord ask if they were ready to go, everyone agreed.

The two couple walked back to the Suites and said goodnight. Linda went to the kitchen to fix Ginger's formulas/ medicines for the night. Marion helped her. Her instructions were very specific and easy to follow. It didn't take them long to finish, label, and put them into the refrigerator.

Marion followed Linda into her suite. Linda said she would love to get into the spa bath. Marion agreed. They went into Linda bathroom and started filling the tub. Linda used the resort products. She decided she was addicted. Linda and Marion were kissing, and he began undressing Linda. She felt so good getting out of the dress she had worn all day. She was also undressing Marion. When they were naked, they both stepped slowly into the bath. Linda just laid back and enjoyed the warmth and the feel of the jets. Marion laid back and enjoyed the view. This was his fantasy.

Linda reminded him that he was going to tell her why he loved her blush. Then he did just that, his voice was low, and he said, "You remember when you were wet and put on that Resort robe, I could see the blush on your face, just like right now. I thought you were the most beautiful women I had ever seen then I looked down, and your breast was nearly covered, and I could see their blush, just like now. I knew then that I wanted you. I wanted to see all of you just like now. I wanted to lay in that bath with you, just like now. Tell me, Linda, what do you want?

Linda started talking low, telling Marion, she wanted more. I want more of your kisses. I want to feel your hands on me and in me. I want more, and I want to feel your manhood in me. I want all of you, and I give you all of me. Marion stepped out of the tub, and he got the Resort robe, and he lifted Linda out of the bathtub and wrapped her in the robe. He stood her in front of the mirror. He was standing behind her. He said, "See the woman I love. You are beautiful. The blush on your face is so naturally beautiful. Now, look at your breast. The blush on your breast makes me want you to touch you". His hands moved over her breast, and the desire ran through her. He held her breast, and he caressed her breast, then he heard her say, I want more. He came around her, and he kissed her lips, they were standing sideways to the mirror, and she could see him. He went to her breast, and he kissed her and sucked her, and she could fill herself wanting more, and she could feel herself getting wet. She watches him tug and suck on her breast until she said I want more. She could feel him hard against her thigh. She could see his hand pull the robe further apart and his hand go to her soft spot. He took in a gulp of air, and he was hard, and straight up, she knew he had discovered that she was soft and wet and there was no hair covering her. He fingered her deep and over and over until she finally yelled, "I want more" Then he carried her to her bed, and he lay on top of her naked, and she said, "I want all of you." Marion started entering her slowly, and she was so wet, she was so tight. He was trying to be easy, and he didn't want to hurt her. Linda pulled him to her and said, "I want all of you." He lost all control if he ever had any, they moved together until he felt her contract and contract again and then he gave her all of him. He felt her contract again, and he knew, he wanted all of her all the time. Good or bad, whatever was to come. He knew he would never let her go. His feelings were so strong and possessive he was afraid to tell her. Before Linda fell asleep, she said, "Marion, I love you, too."

They woke up twice during the night. Neither one said anything they just enjoyed loving each other and feeling the love. They were one now. Linda knew that she wanted Marion. She wanted all of him, all the time whatever was to come good or bad, but she was afraid to say anything.

The next morning Linda heard Marion get up and get in the shower. He was in her shower. She was smiling when she joined him in the shower. They kissed, and he said I was trying to let you sleep in. She said I'll sleep after you leave. He took her right there against the shower wall. He tried to hold back until he felt her contract, but she was just so sexy and so willing. He had to let go, and when he did, he felt her contract again and again. When they recover, they finished their showers, and she slips on a T-shirt dress and went into the kitchen and started the coffee. While the coffee was brewing, she started mixing Ginger's formulas/ medicines. She was finished when he came in dressed and set down. She handed him a cup of coffee and got her one and set down.

He asks her what her plans were, and she said she was free all day. He said he would check back with her at noon. They kissed, and he left.

She called the desk and asked if they could send someone up to her suite. Thank goodness each door had its number like 101A, 101B, so she didn't have to wake the whole household. They came right away, and she had them change the bed and clean the bath. She asks for additional towels and 2 robes. They were very accommodating. They were out of her suite in less than 10 minutes, then she ordered breakfast. She ate a healthy breakfast then put her tray outside the door and rang room service to pick it up.

She put on a robe and climbed into bed, At 11:00, she was awoken by Marion. He was smiling when he saw her in the robe. Then she said, "I want more." He was happy to give her what she wanted. When they were both spent, she said, "What about your lunch." That's when he told her, they had all day. When they walked out the front door, the limousine was there waiting. They got in, and he took her to one of the highest points in San Francisco where they could look back down on the city. They ate a long and luxurious lunch, then headed back to the city. They loved touching each other, and everyone could see the love.

They went down to the wharf and walked through shops and art galleries. They loved every minute. They were in love with life. A little before sunset, they went into one of the restaurants on the wharf. He gave his name, and they escorted Marion and Linda to a window table where they could watch the sunset. They ate seafood and sourdough bread. They talked about the past present and future.

Linda felt she was beautiful for the first time in her life. Even though she had many many honors in high school and her career, her mother had been a critical woman. Her husband was very competitive, and whenever Linda was given honor or award, he would one-up her with a story of his own. She would have never divorced him, but it turns out he died after a short illness.

Now she had Marion, and he said all the right words she had worked and waited and wanted her mother or her husband to say. She was absorbing them like a sponge. She also knew Marion meant it because he liked to show her.

That night when they got back to the suite. Linda went straight to the kitchen to fix Ginger's formulas/medicines. Linda was organized and efficient, and it didn't take her long. Marion was already in bed naked. Linda slowly undressed while Marion watched. She didn't disappoint, and she was blushing from head to toe. She climbed under the covers with Marion. Marion said, "There is something I've never done, and I would like your permission. ". Linda said, "I'm listening." Marion said, "You're the first girl that I've ever seen that doesn't have any hair, down there. That is what I would like to explore." Linda was blushing when she said, "You will be the first." That was all Marion needed to hear. He started with Linda's lips and worked his way down her body. He was amazed at how her body responded to him. She was wet, and he wanted to taste her. He nibbled on the right spots, and he could hear her moan. He used his tongue and fingers, and she cried out. Then he heard her say. Thank you, and she contracted and contracted and contracted. She thought it would never end, and he told her later it was six times. Then he wanted to suck her until she was dry. She was so swollen and sensitive; she had to muffle a scream. She fell asleep exhausted.

When she woke it was morning, he was fully dressed. He woke her to kiss her goodbye. She started blushing, and he kissed her some more. He told her she did not have to get up, and he had fixed all of Ginger's formulas/medicines. He told her he used to help fix them all the time, and he knew what he was doing. They had a long kiss goodbye, and Marion left the suite. She jumped out of bed, grabbed a robe, and went to the refrigerator to double check. Sure enough, everything was perfect.

She went straight to the bathroom. Well, everything was still there, but it felt like it was turned inside out. She turns on the spa, and this time decided it might be best not to use any products since she was so sensitive. She stayed in the spa for over an hour then wrapped in a robe and climbed into bed. She went right to sleep. Marion came in at 1:00, and Linda was still sleeping. He went in to use the bathroom and saw she had been in the tub. The water was still in it, so he knew she hadn't used any of the products. He was wondering why when it dawned on him. Poor thing. Guess he was too rough. He felt terrible.

He climbed into bed with Linda and held her until he fell asleep. Linda woke up around 3:30, Marion was sleeping beside her with his arm around her. She must have been sleeping soundly for her not to know he climbed in bed. She was watching him sleep when he opened his eyes and was looking back at her. He started apologizing right off, telling her he never intended to hurt her. She was saying that neither one of them knew this might happen. She was the one saying I want more. She told him that she was not bleeding and hadn't been bleeding. She was only swollen and very sensitive. Marion told her they would stay in tonight and order room service. Linda also said to him that she and Adri didn't have anything planned for two days. She would probably be able to walk by then. For some reason, they both started laughing about her not being able to walk.

Linda got up and took another spa bath. Once again, she didn't use products, but the warm water and the jet felt good. Marion took care of her all afternoon. Once again, he fixed Ginger's formulas/medicines. They ordered cheeseburgers and French fries and rented a movie on pay per view. They went to bed early. They were holding each other throughout the night.

The next morning, they got up together and showered and dressed before going into the kitchen. Marion made the coffee while Linda mixed the formulas/medicines for the day, putting them into the soft sided ice chest. Cord and Linda carrying Ginger came out of their suite. Linda loaded the ice chest into the stroller, and they all went to breakfast. They decided to eat off the buffet since there was no line. They were able to be seated immediately. Linda had told Marion earlier that she was good to go. He still seemed to be watching her closely. The conversation was about the day, and everyone was excited and happy. While Adri was telling Cord goodbye, Linda whispered to Marion that she was feeling good, but she would let him check her out thoroughly tonight. She walked off laughing.

Today their tour took them on a ferry to Sausalito where they would eat lunch and shop during the afternoon. On the ferry, Adri told Linda that she had never seen Marion as happy as he had been these last few days. She said she was really glad they were enjoying each other. The day flew by. Adri was able to try on some clothes while Linda held Ginger. Linda used hand disinfectant on her hands before she took Ginger. She knew how careful Adri was. Ginger was an angel, and her eyes watched everything. She had a big smile and little giggle. She was adorable.

When they got back to the Resort, the guys were finished for the day. Marion and Linda volunteered to watch Ginger while Cord and Adri went out. Cord had not been out of the Resort in days. His presentations were complete, and the companies they hosted had purchased the products. During this time, it was the techs who worked with the customers.

Cord and Adri accepted the offer, and Adri got Ginger ready for bed. Cord moved the bassinets into Linda's suite. Linda went ahead and got the Formulas/medicines ready for the night. She set her alarms for the feedings. Marion had done this many times, but this was the first time for Linda.

Linda thought she was ready to resume their physical relationship, but Marion decided one more night would help her heal, and they had a distraction, Ginger. Ginger slept soundly while she was watched over by Linda and Marion. They feed her, and as soon as she was asleep, they decided they needed to sleep.

At 3:00 am, they heard screaming and crying. It was Adri, and she was screaming, no no no. They jumped out of bed and ran to help. Cord was holding Adri, and she was doubled over crying and screaming no. Linda ran and wrapped herself around Adri. Adri stopped screaming but continued to cry. Cord was crying as well neither was able to tell Marion and Linda what had happened. Then Cord's phone rang, Marion, answered. It was security, Marion asks what had happened. He explained that Cord and Adri were so upset they were unable to explain. Security told Marion they would send a doctor.

They said that Mr. and Mrs. Moore had contacted Adri and Cord. They were the parents of JP Moore, Ginger's father, and KD Moore, Ginger's Uncle. They had found out that JP had a daughter, Ginger and they would be coming to pick Ginger up and take her home with them. They were her biological grandparents, and strangers shouldn't raise her. They would raise her. Security said they would fax a copy of the letter.

There was a knock on the door, and it was the doctor. Marion hung up the phone. Linda was talking quietly to Adri. Now that she knew the problem, she was making statements of reassurance to Adri. The doctor gave Adri a sedative, and both Cord and Marion picked her off the floor and carried her to bed. She was already in her pajamas so they must have been woken up with this news. Cord didn't want a sedative, so the doctor gave him a mild sleeping pill to help him sleep.

When Adri and Cord were finally asleep, Marion went to the fax machine. He read the letter. He wanted to cry and scream himself after reading it. Instead, he called Cord's Attorney and told him about the letter. He faxed the attorney a copy as soon as they were off the phone. He told him that Cord and Adri were too upset to deal with this tonight. They would call tomorrow.

THE LETTER

Dear Cord,

We have just found out that JP fathered a child. The child named Ginger that you have been taking care of. We are her biological grandparents, and even though we appreciate you opening your home to her, you are not actually her biological Grandfather. Ginger's mother was your stepdaughter, and you have no biological connection to Ginger's mother or Ginger.

We also understand that you have a lady named Adri living with you, outside of wedlock which my husband and I don't feel is the right environment for Ginger. Once again, we appreciate Adri and her care of Ginger, but we feel that Ginger should be living in our home with her biological Grandparents.

We would also like to say that decorating her bedroom with JP's Art is totally inappropriate. Ginger is just a child and could easily damage JP's Art pieces, which could affect the value. Please have the artwork crated and ready to ship. My husband and I will decide the appropriate venue to display JP's art pieces.

We will be coming to your home within the week to pick up Ginger and bring her home with us. Please pack her things and have her ready.

We also understand that Ginger inherited JP's entire estate, and we expect you to have all the paperwork transferred to my husband and me. We will take over as executors of the inheritance.

Ginger's Biological Grandparents,
Mr. & Mrs. JR Moore

The next morning Linda woke early and went into the kitchen to mix Ginger's formulas medicines for the day. Then she fed and bathed Ginger. She dressed Ginger in one of her many adorable outfits and rocked her to sleep. Marion awoke, and he and Linda quickly showered and dressed. They took Ginger into the Main living area, and Marion ordered breakfast for four. After about 10 minutes Cord and Adri wondered into the living area. Both were still in their pajamas, and both looked like they were defeated.

Linda stood up and hugged them both. She then directed Cord to sit in the corner of a massive sectional. She then directed Adri to sit in Cord's lap. Linda then walked over and took Ginger from Marion and put her in Adri's lap. Linda pulled up a chair, and she was so close she was touching knees with Cord. Linda began, "We have all read this letter and know it's contents. This letter is not a legal document. I want you both to look at me and listen to everything I am about to say. (Cord and Adri looked up at Linda). This letter is not a legal document." "AGREED," Cord and Adri nodded their heads. Linda continued, "The reason for this letter becomes obvious if you read the last paragraph. I quote, "We also understand, and we expect you to have all the paperwork transferred to my husband and I. We will take over as executors of the inheritance," unquote.

Linda said, "This is what JP's parents want, they want the inheritance. To get the inheritance, they have to take Ginger." "AGREED," Cord and Ginger nodded their heads.

Linda continued, "Now that we know what they want, your Attorney will know how to proceed." "AGREED," Cord and Ginger nodded in agreement. Linda said, "Now the rest of the letter are slams, so let's slam back.

"They are correct that you are not Ginger's biological parents or grandparents, BUT you do not have to be connected biologically to be her guardians, to have custody, and or to be the executors. Cord you have the papers and video of Ginger's mother giving you full custody of Ginger. Those custody papers were witnessed and signed by a Judge and filed in court. Adri you have pictures and video of the 'Sip and See' that JP held in his home. JP repeatedly says that God has blessed him with Ginger. Then God continued to bless him by giving Ginger two guardian angels, Cord and Adri. God, triple blessed him. He goes on to say that he is overjoyed that these two wonderful people will raise Ginger. JP signed papers giving you, Cord, and you, Adri, legal custody of Ginger. These papers were included with the Inheritance papers and had been signed by a Judge and filed in court. The papers are legal, and these videos will stand up in court. "AGREED," this time Cord and Adri both said yes yes yes.

Linda continued, "They also slammed you about hanging JP's Art in Ginger's room. Well, if I remember correctly, the artist the brothers sent to hang the artwork had FaceTime with JP and KD throughout. In addition to that, you have a photographer videoing and another taking a picture of the process. It was evident that both brothers wanted the art hung in Ginger's room. The best part though was Cord video of Ginger's reaction to the art". "AGREED." Cord and Adri said again yes yes yes. Then Adri asks Linda how she knew all this. Linda told her that she had gone through tons of pictures and viewed hours of video as soon as she found out Ginger would be her patient. She wanted to know everything she could about Ginger". Adri stood up and hugged Linda and squashed Ginger in the middle. Adri said, "JP has been blessed again with another guardian angel for Ginger." There were tears in everyone's eyes, but they were happy tears.

Cord said, "There is one more slam, and I can handle this one. I ask Adri to marry me, and she accepted, but we decided our focus was on Ginger for as long as we were blessed with her so we would wait to plan a wedding. We both feel that we are already joined as one in the site of God. Matter of fact, we have been seeing our minister for counseling. ". Then Cord turned to Adri and said, "Adri, are you ready to marry me?" Adri answered, "Yes!" Then pulled her necklace out of her pajamas and hanging on the necklace was a beautiful diamond ring. Adri took the ring off the necklace and Cord put it on her finger. The room came alive with congratulations and best wishes.

Then Cord got everyone's attention and said, "Adri and I have chosen a location in Hawaii, and I called the minister this morning, and he and his wife are ready to go. We are all flying to Hawaii for our wedding! Pack up, be ready to go by noon". Everyone scrabbled, and by noon, they were walking out the front door of the resort. Marion and Linda got into the front seat and Cord, Adri, and Ginger got in the back of the limousine and headed toward the airport.

When everything was loaded, and the plane was in the air headed for Hawaii, Cord, Adri, and Ginger moved across the aisle to the two seats facing Marion and Linda. Cord asked Marion and Linda if they would stand up with them as their best man and bridesmaid and also sign as witnesses for their marriage. Marion and Linda were honored to accept, and there were hugs all around.

The girls immediately started talking about what they were wearing. Cord looked at Marion and said, "I've got you a tuxedo, how about we open some champagne." They left the girls to their planning. Adri explained that she had already found her dress and had it sized plus at the same time she had found the dress she would like Linda to wear. She said the dress was gold and she knew Linda's size from their shopping so it should fit. Then she told Linda that she even had Ginger's dress picked out. She said she had seen it in a Children's shop at home, but she hadn't bought it, but the minister's wife had already gone by the shop and picked it up with matching shoes and everything. We will all be carrying deep red rose bouquets. Adri said, "We are all set."

The plane ride to Hawaii was a celebration. They ate and watched romance movies and ate and played cards and ate and ate and ate. Adri and Linda began to wonder if their dresses would still fit.

They arrived in Hawaii, and there was a limousine and driver waiting for them. They headed to the resort, and when they walked in the front door, they were greeted by the minister and his wife. They were shown to their Suites, and everything was luxurious. Linda and Marion were in the same suite. Marion had requested it earlier when he was with Cord. They were both pleased. The time was all mixed up, and it was still nighttime in Hawaii. They all decided to get a few hours' sleep and meet for breakfast.

Cord and Adri's Suite adjoined Marion's and Linda's. Linda unpacked Ginger's formulas and medicines and organized everything. She ignored the time difference and kept Ginger on the same schedule. She fixed enough to get through the night. She could see Adri and Cord were still unpacking, so she knocked on the open door of their suite and Adri came to greet her and thank her. She asks if she could help unpack Ginger's things, but Adri told her she and Cord had it down to a fine science, it wouldn't take them any time. Linda said goodnight and headed to her suite.

Marion had unpacked both his and Linda's things and had two bathrobes laying on the bed when Linda came into the suite. Linda started laughing, and Marion said, "There's a spa tub." They headed to the bathroom and started filling the tub. They used the Resort products and climbed into the tub to relax. They stayed in the tub nearly an hour before Marion climbed out, put on a robe and helped Linda climb out and wrapped Linda in a robe and carried her to bed. Once they were in bed, they were busy pleasing one another and soon they were joined as one.

What they would never know was that in the adjoining suite, Cord and Adri were following the same routine. The two couple were more alike than they knew.

The next morning was the morning of the wedding. Everyone was excited at breakfast. Adri laid out the schedule for everyone. The wedding was scheduled for 4 in the afternoon. The three ladies were going to spend the day at the spa. Adri had scheduled the royal treatment. They would have facials, massages, manicures, pedicures, lunch at the spa then hair and makeup. They would take Ginger with them. They would dress at the spa then a limousine would pick them up at the spa at 3:30. The ladies loved every minute of their spa treatment. The minister's wife, Stacey fit in instantly with Adri and Linda. She had a positive and fun attitude.

The three men were going to play golf and have lunch at the golf course clubhouse. Then they would come back to the resort and get ready. A limousine would pick them up at the Resort Entrance at 3:30.

The setting for the wedding was actually on the resort. Even though Adri was telling everyone the plans for the day, there was a wedding planner with the ladies. The wedding planner also had someone with the men.

Everyone enjoyed the day, and at 3:30, three handsome men in black tuxedos walked across the lobby and out the front entrance. They were so handsome, young and older women stopped what they were doing to get a good long look. The men laughed at something, and the women watching could be heard sighing. They were the most handsome three men in the resort.

The wedding planner was taking special care to make sure the ladies' makeup and hair was perfect. She and her assistant helped each lady get into their dress. Before Adri got into her dress, she dressed Ginger. Ginger looked like a beautiful baby doll. The gold was a perfect color for her. She had deep red roses at the breast of her gold dress and on the band around her head. The deep red and gold in her hair were surrounded by Ginger colored curls. The hues of the colors were perfect together. The minister's wife was going to hold Ginger during the service until the point that her husband asks her to bring her forward.

Linda and Stacey loved their dresses. They were made of the same gold material as Ginger's, but each was designed to flatter both ladies' figures. Adri had learned about style and design while she and Ginger were staying with JP. There were slight differences that most probably wouldn't notice. Adri thought both ladies looked beautiful. They both had the deep red roses woven in their hair when they looked into the mirror; they both decided their hair had never looked better or flatter them as much as today. They both took out their phone and started clicking pictures from every direction. Adri was laughing the whole time. Of course, everyone expects the bride to look beautiful, and Adri did not disappoint. Adri was gorgeous! Just like each ladies dress was the most flattering for them, now each lady's hair was done in the most flattering for them and accented with deep red roses.

Then it was Adri's turn. She stepped into her dress, and when she pulled the dress up, she looked into the mirror. She loved the dress. She had forgotten how beautiful the dress was with details everywhere she looked. Then she looked up from the dress and saw herself. She felt beautiful. She looked beautiful. She could not believe how the dress transformed her. She couldn't wait to see Cord and for him to see her.

The ladies were full of compliments for Adri and each other. It was going to be a wonderful day; they all felt beautiful. They walk out of the spa and into the waiting limousine. The wedding planner said it would only take 2 or 3 minutes to get to their destination and the men were there waiting. Stacey asks if she could say a prayer, and Adri nodded to her. It was a lovely prayer of blessings on this day, blessings on Adri, and blessings on this marriage. It was perfect, and as she ended; they pull up to the most beautiful place on earth.

They couldn't see the men. A beautiful garden separated them. They could see a walkway dividing the garden, and everything was blooming. Music from a string quartet begins playing. The wedding planner signaled Stacey, who was holding Ginger to go first. Stacey was holding Ginger cradled in her arm where Ginger was sitting up with her head on Stacey's shoulder. Ginger was alert and looking around. Stacey walked to where the gardens divided and turned up the walkway. She had to stop to take in the beauty of what she was seeing. On both sides of the walkway, there were walls of deep red roses leading to the altar where they connected with a wall of deep red roses behind the altar. She could not believe her eyes. Her husband was standing in front of a wall of red roses. She knew that Cord and Marion were standing there with her husband, but she only had eyes for her husband as she walked among the roses with the beautiful music playing. She walked up and stood next to her husband as she had been directed. Ginger large blue eyes were opened wide, and she smiled when she saw Cord. Next Linda started walking, and when she turned up the walkway, she knew immediately why Stacey had stopped. She realized she had stopped as well. The roses covered walls that must have been seven feet high. Every rose was perfect, and you couldn't tell where one ended, and another started and the fragrance.

Linda had never seen anything as beautiful. Marion was watching Linda, and he couldn't take his eyes away from her. Marion was very moved; Stacey saw him wipe a tear from his eye. Linda looked so beautiful! She took her place opposite from Marion. Then the music changed, and the string quartet started playing the traditional wedding march. Adri came into view. She paused, she looked at the deep red rose walls and thought perfect, she looked at her friends, and her thought was perfect. Then her eyes looked directly at Cord and started walking toward him. Linda and Stacey were both thinking she was the most beautiful bride they had ever seen, and Stacey had seen a lot of brides.

The white bridal dress sparkled as she walked, and the sun caught the crystals. It was magical. Cord could not look away from Adri. She was the most beautiful lady he had ever seen. Her dress was beautiful, but he couldn't look away from her gorgeous face. He had known for months that she was beautiful inside and out and was proud that she had chosen him. Now, as she came toward him, he was thinking she has chosen me, and it nearly brought him to his knees. He felt like he was the luckiest man on earth.

When Adri started down the path, she immediately saw Cord. She knew she loved him. She loved so many things about him. Now, as she looked at him, she was thinking, 'how I got so lucky that this handsome man loves me, too.' She couldn't take her eyes off him. He looked so handsome and so happy. When she stepped up beside him, he took her hand and whispered. "I love you." They both turned toward the minister, but Ginger caught their attention. She appeared so alert, looking directly at Adri and Cord. Her big blue eyes were opened wide, and her little smile touched their hearts.

The minister began with a prayer of blessing for Adri and Cord and their uniting before God and man. He read scripture. Then Adri handed her bridal bouquet of red roses to Linda, and Marion handed her the wedding band. Adri placed the wedding band on Cord's finger as she recited her vows. Then Marion handed Cord two rings that were circles of diamonds that he placed on Adri's finger as he recited his vows. Then the minister said, "You are now united as one in the sight of God and man." "You may kiss your bride." Cord wrapped his arms around Adri and tipped her back in a very romantic kiss.

When the kiss was over, and Cord was holding Adri upright, the minister reached for Ginger and placed her in Adri's arms, immediately Cord wrapped his arm around Adri's arm helping her hold Ginger close. The minister continued, "This little angel, Ginger, has blessed both you, Adri, and you, Cord, by bringing you two into each other's lives. You both have blessed Ginger by accepting, without hesitation, the roles as Ginger's Guardian Angels". Then the minister prayed for many blessings to continue to abound in this family.

The minister introduced Cord and Adri as husband and wife and asked everyone to join them. The string quartet became playing as Cord, Adri, and Ginger led them back down the path through the rose walls and in the opposite direction from where the ladies had entered the garden. They had only gone a short distance on the garden path when they came upon a waterfall. They all stopped at the waterfall and admired God's artwork. It was magnificent.

Cord, Adri, and Ginger led them to a naturally made alcove. In the Alcove, was a golden semicircle booth large enough to accommodate all six of them easily. Adri, Ginger & Cord set in the middle, then on one side was Stacey and her husband and the other side Linda and Marion were seated. Their view was of a large sandy beach and beautiful crystal blue water, as far as they could see. Native Hawaiians immediately started serving them drinks in decorated coconuts. They were told the drink was called Hawaiian Mama, Stacey asks one of the servers what was in a Hawaiian Mama. The server put his finger to his temple and thought, then said, "A Hawaiian Papa." They were all laughing as Native Dancers and Story Tellers appeared. The evening was transformed by delicious Native Hawaiian Dishes and the entertainment. They ended the evening by making wishes and setting hot air balloons into the night. The couple stood on the beach and watched until they could no longer see the Hot Air Balloons. The wedding planner led them to their limousine. As they all said their goodbyes to the wedding planner, Cord discretely handed her an envelope. She was to find out later when she opened the envelope that there was cash equal to the amount of the bill Cord had paid when booking the Wedding Planner and event. He had given her not 15%, not 20% but a 100% tip. Her eyes filled with tears.

In the limousine on the way back to the Resort, Cord announced that he and Adri had planned excursions for the next six days and they wanted both couples to join them. He told them that they had been having so much fun together; they had decided that they wanted to share their honeymoon. Everyone was thrilled. Just as they were entering the resort, Adri said for everyone to wear cool, comfortable clothes and shoe the next day. They would meet at 9:00 for breakfast. The next morning everyone met, and that began days of snorkeling, touring on Segway's, island hopping by plane, touring gardens, touring plantations, romantic dinners on the beach at sunset, touring Pearl Harbor, visiting 6 Polynesian villages, a trip in a glass bottom boat. A Dinner Cruise. Tours of Naval ships in the harbor. Ginger went everywhere with them. The day they snorkeled. They were hosted in the home of a longtime Hawaii resident. She volunteered to watch Ginger while the couples snorkeled. To surprise Adri and Cord, she set up a video to record her activities with Ginger. Adri cried when her host gave her the disc.

When everyone boarded Cords plane to return home, they were happily exhausted. All three couples were returning together. It was a mutual decision that this would not be goodbye. They would be lifelong friends.

Cord talked to security once he was on the plane headed home. They reported that Mr. and Mrs. JR Moore had shown up at Cord's home, fully expecting to pick up Ginger and get their hands on her inheritance. Security met them at the door and reported that Cord, Adri, and Ginger were not home. The Moore's told security that they had contacted Cord, they were coming. Security asks them how they contacted Cord (knowing already), and they both responded by mail. It was then that security showed the Moore's a stack of mail on the entry table. They pulled out their letter (which had been sealed and put there on purpose). The Moore's were told that obviously Cord had not gotten the letter yet and Cord would contact them when he got home and received the mail. They were furious. They even started arguing with each other because they were depending on THAT money to pay for their hotel and their travel expense. They didn't have money to return home. They didn't even have money for meals. They decided they would eat at their motel until Cord got home. Then Mrs. Moore realized that their motel had a spa. She perked up and told her husband, and she would spend her time having full beauty treatment. (They said all this in front of security as if he wasn't there). He opened the door for them, and they left.

When Adri, Ginger, Cord, Marion, and Linda arrived at home. They were met at the door by security and Cord' Attorney. Their time was messed up by the difference in time zones, Hawaiian time. So, they all sit down in Cord's study. The security had five cameras on the visit from Mr. And Mrs. JR Moore. They had put the footage of each camera into a program that coordinated the footage and gave them a panoramic view. The security starts the recording of the visit on the 80" screen TV that is in Cord's office. Everyone that had been sitting comfortably in the massive leather furniture now set forward on the edge of their seats. Security played the recording three times. Everyone got the message loud and clear. The Moore's were breaking they needed to get their hands on Ginger's inheritance as soon as possible.

Everyone in the room voiced their opinion on how to proceed with Mr. and Mrs. Moore.

After 3 hours, they were all in agreement as to how they would proceed. Cord called the Moore's at their hotel. He talked to JR, Mrs. Moore was getting her hair colored in the salon and was not available. Cord ask him if they could come the next day at 3:00 pm. JR was very agreeable.

Linda fixed Ginger's formulas/medicines, and everyone retired to their suites to rest and acclimate to the time zone. They each knew the role they would play tomorrow. There was some reviewing and rehearsing involved. The chef and her helpers kept a buffet set out for the household since everyone seemed to be trying to rest but also reviewing thick folders of information.

The next day everyone returned to the study at 2:30. This time they all set around the conference table. They left two seats open at the end of the conference table for Mr. and Mrs. JR Moore. There wasn't much talking, and everyone was prepared. The one person that was not present was Ginger. She was in the safest place in the home. She was on the second floor with 3 of the security team. She was sound asleep.

The JR Moore's showed up early. The family had predicted they would because they needed the money. The research that had been done in the last 24hours proved how desperate they were. They had no income. Even their home was in foreclosure, and it had a second mortgage against it, that was also being foreclosed. They had been living on credit cards, and those were maxed to the limit.

The Head of security led them to the conference table and showed them to the last two seats. The family lawyer was sitting at the opposite end. Linda and Marion were on their left and Cord, and Adri was on their right. The Attorney began by saying that we needed to start by clearing up a few matters.

Cord began by looking directly into Moore's eyes, and he told them that they did not know him. "You do not know my family, and you do not know my business, if you continue to slander anyone in my family or my wife Adri, I will proceed with litigation against you." Well, this wasn't the direction the Moore's thought this meeting would be going. Cord was staining down JR Moore. JR turned to his wife and said, I told you not to put something like that in writing. You need to apologize right now". Mrs. JR Moore turned as red as her new hair color. She softly said, "I'm sorry." Cord said I don't think Adri heard you. He then stared down Mrs. Moore. She said, "Adri, I'm sorry."

Never taking his eyes off them both, Cord continued, "I would also like to make it crystal clear to both you, that a person does not need to have a biological connection to a child to be a guardian. To have custody, to adopt, or to be an executor of an estate. The Moore's started to shift in their chairs. JR said, "Well Judges usually like to see children with their biological family." Mrs. Moore said, "Yeah, that's right." Cord said, "Well, you may find that you're going to have a problem getting a Judge ever to hear you. I told you, YOU do not know my family".

Adri handed two thick folders to the Moore's. Adri said, "You might want to find out about your biological son, JP. The son you kicked out of your home when he was 15 for loving someone. You kicked him out of your house with only the clothes on his back. You canceled his tuition for the private school you had selected. The son you said was dead to you. You never knew JP. You never recognized his talent as an artist, and you never recognized his educational genius.

JP went to your neighbors and used their phone. What you don't know is that the neighbors were glad to see JP get out from under your control. Their worry now was for KD left in the house. JP made one phone call. It was to the administration of one of the top Schools of Arts and Science. They had received his application earlier that day. They immediately offered him a full scholarship. The application showed that your 15-year-old son had not only completed all the advanced classes offered with the highest scores but had also completed three-semester courses. He had declared a double major of Bachelor of Arts and Sciences and Bachelors of Chemical Engineer. The School of Arts and Science recognized immediately that this student could raise their academic ratings and they jumped at the opportunity. JP told them he needed to transfer today, and he also would like to be assigned a suite tonight. He did not want roommates or suitemates. The administration met all his needs. As they were leaving him to move into his suite, they laughing said, "Do you by any chance have any siblings"?

JP stopped and turn to look at the team assigned him. He said, "I do have one brother, but I won't be 16 until next week. At that time, we have an appointment to go before a Judge and ask for me to be made his guardian". "He is 13, and he is an artist as well interested in Engineering. I'm aware you have never taken a student that young, but he has also already completed the advanced courses. He can also provide grades that will increase your school's academic levels". They said they were very interested in looking at his school records. JP said he could get the records if someone could drive him to his workshop or the bus line. The team all jumped into a University vehicle. They drove to the wharf, and JP unlocked the door. He went into an office area and got records out of the file cabinet.

The administration team could not believe the building was three stories high. The lighting was awesome, and the art pieces, some completed, some in the process. The Art Department Administrator said, "I recognize your work. You have already had two art exhibits that I have attended. Your pieces of artwork at your shows has gone for six figures, and I understand your commissioned work is in the millions". JP said that is how we afford to rent to own this workshop. The administrator asked, "Are the metal pieces your brothers"? JP answered, "Yes, now you see why he is interested in Engineering."

One of the administrators had continued through the office area and had seen a large modern kitchen with all amenities and the two king size bedrooms with big screen TV. When he came out, he wanted to know why JD wanted a suite at the school. JD said, "The previous owners had just remodeled, and we kept them like they were because sometimes we work through the night on our art. The bedrooms were our back-up plan as well if we didn't get scholarships".

As JP was locking up, he said, "This will be your only visit to our workshop. Our art pieces are our visions. We have purchased this workshop to maintain secrecy until we exhibited the art. I would like for you to keep what you have seen today confidential. We don't even want the address known". They all agreed. They would never betray these two brothers.

JP' brother's record was exemplary. When KD turned 16, he went before the Judge and after the Judge saw what these boys had accomplished while living in prison with their parents as the wardens. He had made his decision, even before the neighbors and the administration from the Private School testified. JP was appointed a legal guardian of his brother.

They celebrated by going to buy JP a new pickup, a King Ranch. They then went clothes shopping. Their Mother had chosen their clothes their whole lives. Thank goodness the private school required uniforms, or they would have been the brunt of every joke. They were glad to leave with only the shirts on their back. They had bought clothes that were necessary to use in creating their art, but today they focused on their clothes for school. JP chose more Preppy clothes and KD chose more beach bum T-shirt's and wild shorts, but of good quality. Then they went to their favorite spot to eat double meat cheeseburgers and cheese fries. The owner recognized them and gave them the booth with the most light. Then he handed JP a 44 oz Coke and KD a 44 oz Water. They celebrated their freedom.

Mr. and Mrs. Moore looked board, but Adri continued. She knew the brother background by heart. KD had his first Art Show and was very successful. He sold all his pieces for at least six figures. JP was very proud of him. There was always an open bar at the Art Shows, but neither brother drank (they weren't old enough), but the host put JD's coke on ice and KD's water on ice in crystal glasses. That became the norm at all their future shows.

JP had been supporting KD up until KD's first show. Then JP gave him his ledger and KD kept his books. They only used accountants to help with their taxes. KD made safes, some that were hidden in pieces of art, some that were hidden in furniture and all had different puzzles to open them. At first, they kept most of their cash at their shop. They installed their security cameras.

They both settled into school, and their art was becoming very popular. They decided they were lonely, especially JP. He had lost his love. His love didn't want their relationship to become public. JP suggested to KD that they buy homes, even though they were openly gay. They liked to keep their romances private. They went online and studied the areas of town that were considered the safest. They ended up purchasing enough property to build two gated estates. JP was 18, and KD was 15 when they built their first homes. They hired the same contractor and different decorators. They had lots of fun! Their house plans were the same, their kitchen was laid out the same, their appliances were the same, and everything was the top of the line. Even though they hired decorators, they worked closely with them—they're personally shown through.

The first man JP brought to his home was the administrator over the Engineering Programs on the Naval base. They were a great fit, and while they were together, they remained exclusive. They still preferred to party in the gay community from time to time. But they especially enjoyed their time together alone.

While they were together, the Engineering Department had come up against a problem they couldn't solve. Colonel Wright knew that JP or KD might be able to help, but he could not bring the information off base, he couldn't even talk to them about it. But he could hire consultants and bring them onto the base. That's what he decided to do. The Col. picked them up one evening, and on the way to the base, he told them what he was doing. They were both excited and willing to help. They had to wear visitor badges and had to sign paper after paper, mainly about confidentiality. They knew the importance of confidentiality and signed willingly. They were given the problem and a well-lighted desk to work at. They were both assigned the same desk but worked separately. KD said, "look at this", and JP said, "look at this". They traded papers and said in unison. "That works." The Col heard them and came over to look at their work, and he told them to put both solutions on the board. They did, and the class was amazed. Both solutions worked, and they were different approaches. The class invited JP and KD to go out with them for beers. The bothers just laughed. The Col told the class they were too young to buy beer. KD and JP walked out the door of the quiet classroom.

JP and KD wouldn't take any compensation, and they were happy to help. The Col. continued to show up and kidnap them a time or two a year. Even after he and JP had made a mutual decision to go their separate ways.

When KD turned 16, JP bought him a King Ranch Pickup and filled the truck bed with bottled water and covered it with a tarp and threw a big bow on it. When he came into the workshop and said, "What have you done," as he pulled the tarp off. JP said, You never have enough water to keep hydrated, welding as much as you do". "I meant, what have you done!" "I wanted a Porsche?" JP pushed the garage door opener as they both heard the engines of two Porsche pulling in the workshop. JP said, "Which one do you want"? KD walked over and climbed into the Red Porsche and took off. JP ran to the Black Porsche and took off after him.

By the time JP was 21, he had earned a Doctorate in Chemical Engineering with a second Doctorate in Art Sciences. KD had completed his Masters in Engineering with a second Masters in Arts Sciences and was beginning his Doctorate Studies. They continued their studies and maintained the lifestyle they had been living, focusing on their art. They were becoming very wealthy. They decided that as soon as KD completed his Doctorate Studies, they would travel.

KD completed his Doctorate in Engineering and also received a Doctorate in Art Sciences. They had planned to travel across the United States then travel to Europe. They traveled First Class. Their reputations as Artist opened doors in all the Major Cities. They made instant friends in the Art communities as well as the Gay communities. They were enjoying life. The never developed any taste for beer or liquor. They continued to enjoy their Coke and Water. They also never smoked cigarettes or marijuana or hooked up with anyone that did because they were Artist and didn't want the smoke around their art.

It was during their travels that JP met Doug, another renowned Artist. Doug traveled with JP and KD throughout Europe. Doug wanted JP to move into his home as soon as they arrived back into San Francisco. KD agreed, and he had witnessed the love between the two men throughout their travels through Europe. KD and JP were both ready to get back to San Francisco and back to work on their art.

The sons you rejected settled back in San Francisco and became World Renown Artist and both accumulated great wealth. There came a time when Doug became very hurt because he was not allowed to enter the brother's workshop or even view the art until it was on public display. Around that same time, the brothers had been invited to Aspen, Colorado. They both enjoyed snow skiing and had become quite accomplished while in Switzerland. They accepted the invitation, and it was on that trip that Debbie offered herself a challenge to both brothers that she could change their preference for men because every man she had ever been with had come back for more. All placed the bets in the skiing party, gay or straight. The brothers decided to go along to avoid the fight that was brewing. JP received a call from Doug the very next morning. He told JR that he couldn't live without him and he would accept the confidentiality JP demanded. For them, it was love til Death did them part. JP charted a flight and headed back to San Francisco immediately."

JR Moore interrupted, "Well, you have left out their lifestyle, and they're both contracting AIDS. You think we want our lives to end up like theirs. They deserve what they got."

Adri broke down crying. Cord caught her as she was doubling over into the floor. He said,"

We are taking a break. It might be better if you both stay in the study. I will send refreshments." Everyone but Mr. and Mrs. Clark got up from the conference table and left the room, with tears in their eyes and running down their cheeks.

They all realized the Moore's were unaware that Ginger had AIDS. AIDS was a virus, not a punishment for lifestyle.

Cord made sure the Moore's were served refreshments. He also made sure security stayed in the conference room with them. JR began talking as soon as the others left the room. first. He was saying, "They think we don't know JP accumulated large amounts of wealth, that's why we are here. How much longer are they going to drag this out? I'm ready to get the money and split this place". Mrs. Moore said, "Show me the money." Neither one ever even mentioned Ginger.

While gathered around the dining table, a plan was laid out, and everyone agreed. When they walked back into the Conference Room, Adri was carrying Ginger. Linda had mixed the formula/medicines. Adri said, "Mrs. Moore, would you like to feed Ginger?" It was obvious

Mrs. Moore did not, but after stuttering around without coming up with an excuse. Adri place Ginger in Mrs. Moore's arms. There was a sigh around the table, this was the hardest part of the plan, and they were afraid Adri would not be able to do it.

Mrs. Moore said, "You haven't been feeding this child enough. At nine months, she should be on whole milk and table food." Adri jumped out of her chair and stood glaring at Mrs. Moore. Then Adri said, "How would you know what is best for Ginger?" "When JP introduced Ginger to his friends and family in his home at the Sip and See, 542 guests were in attendance. I know for a fact you both were invited. Where was your concern and care for your Biological Granddaughter?

"Then again, at JP's Memorial Service, the Funeral Chapel was filled with 880 friends and family. With hundreds of mourners outside." "Where was your concern and care about your Biological Granddaughters future?"

"We are all aware that you showed no concern or care for your Biological Granddaughter until

People Magazine published an article about the World's Wealthiest Baby, Ginger Moore."

JR said, "You can't prove that."

Linda stood up slowly as Adri set down. Linda began, "Don't be so sure. I want to introduce myself. I am Ginger's nutritionist. I am responsible for Ginger getting the most current nutrients and medicines for her condition. Ginger is on a variety of formulas that are constantly changing based on her current needs and the most up to date medical information. Ginger is on a schedule of medications that are given as frequently as every two hours."

Mrs. Moore chimed in, "Well, what you are doing is not working. if you think we are going to hire you to continue starving our Biological Granddaughter, you are crazy."

Linda calmly said, "If you think I would ever work for you. You are crazy. Ginger requires a regiment of nutrients and medication because this INNOCENT CHILD was born with the AIDS virus". Linda was leaning over Mrs. Moore, and as Mrs. Moore let go to drop Ginger, Linda was ready to cuddle Ginger. Mrs. Moore shouted, "You have contaminated me." JR shouted, "No amount of money could convince us to raise this child." Linda said, "So the amount of money was what you cared and were concerned about?" "Not your Biological Granddaughter."

Cord stood up and said, "The first thing I told you was that you did not know me! You do not know the love my family has for Ginger. We have taken every precaution to care and protect Ginger". The family attorney stood up and directed everyone to view the large TV screen. Debbie's face filled the screen. She was saying that she did not want Sissy, Ginger. She had never wanted children, and she still didn't want children. She went on to say that she wanted Cord to be the guardian, custodian, or adopted parent. She was willing to sign all the papers necessary. She would give up her parental rights for Cord to adopt Ginger. Debbie signed the necessary documents, the Judge signed, the witnesses signed, the notary signed. The attorney said he would file the papers at the Court House the very next morning.

Then Steve came into view and said, "If My DNA proves I'm Ginger's Biological Father. I want

Cord to be her guardian, her custodian, or adopted parent. I want to sign all the papers necessary. I want to give up my parental rights in order for Cord to adopt her". The DNA came back, showing that Steve was not Ginger's Biological Parent. The papers, Steve signed were destroyed. They were never filed at the Court House.

The video was changed, and JP's face filled the screen. JP was carrying Ginger from room to room. It was the day of the "Sip and See." When JP walked into the rooms, everyone would get quiet, and JP would say," God blessed me with this little angel, Ginger." "I have been thankful for every minute, that I have been given with her." "Then God blessed me by giving Ginger two guardian angels, Cord and Adri." "God has tripled blessed me." "I want everyone to know my wishes." "I am signing all the documents that are required by law that are necessary for Ginger's Guardian Angels to have custody to watch over my angel *Ginger" and continue to love her and care for her, all the days of my life until death do us part." It would be my sincere hope and prayer for Ginger that Cord and Adri adopt her and continue their love and care of her". Then In front of JP's friends and family, he signed all the legal documents necessary, A Judge signed, then two witnessed signed, and the papers were notarized for the attorney to file at the Court House the next morning.

Cord looked directed at JR Moore and Mrs. Moore. "As you can see, Debbie and JP gave their legal consent, documented on video, signed by a Judge, and recorded at the Court House. You can never be a part of Ginger's life. You are banned from this home and any properties we own just as you ban your sons JP and KD.

The attorney stood and handed two papers to the Moore's. "You are being served: You are now being served with a cease and desist order as well as a protective order, you are never to contact or come within 500 yards of Ginger."

Cord added, "Ginger has a full team of security. You will never see her again. You will never have a chance to poison her in any way against JP."

Then Linda did something no one in the room was prepared for. Linda followed the Moore's to the door. At the door, Linda lowered her voice and said to Mr. and Mrs. JR Moore, "You might want to burn your clothes. You might want to shave your heads. You might want to bath in at least 25% Clorox plus water. If you are concerned about contamination". As the Moore's ran for their car, Linda yelled, "Try not to contaminate your car or house."

When Linda walked back into the conference room, everyone was applauding! The next day at the checkout counters, one magazine's front-page story was accompanied by a full-length picture of JR Moore and his wife in the front yard of their home naked and burning their clothes while shaving their heads. The next picture was of them lighting their car on fire. The police arrived and arrested them. It was reported that they were yelling about needing a Clorox bath, something about contamination. They were both still mumbling about a Clorox bath when the police admitted them to the Psychiatric Ward of the nearest hospital for a seven-day evaluation. It was reported that the only way the staff could get them to quiet down was to give them baths with Clorox. (NOT the staff emptied Clorox bottles and filled with water)

After seven days the staff reported that JR Moore and Mrs. Moore were so delusional, they continued to think they were contaminated and insisted upon a routine of shaving their hair and bathing in Clorox baths clean new sheets. The staff recommended permanent hospital admission and continued treatment for their delusions. The hospital Staff never connected their delusions to AIDS. They both tested negative to the AIDS Virus and because the answers the Moore's had given on their questionnaires showed they had not been exposed to the virus. It was common knowledge that AIDS was not transferred in any manner they had filled out on their questionnaires. It was later learned that both JR and Mrs. Moore were heavily sedated to keep them from harming themselves.

Over the years as Mr. JR Moore and Mrs., Moore was evaluated the consensus of the Psychiatric Teams continued to conclude that the Moore's fears and delusions had kept them from enjoying a life that included their very intelligent and artistic sons.

After the Moore's left, Cord, Adri, Ginger, Linda, and Marion were elated but emotionally drained. Linda and Marion went directly to the kitchen to mix Ginger's nutrients and medications. They instinctively knew that Cord and Adri would want to spend a quiet evening with their angel, Ginger.

Ginger had her next scheduled doctor visited the following week. Ginger's doctor and health team agreed that Ginger had gained enough weight to try adding two more ounces of formula and try feedings every three hours. Linda would be communicating with Ginger's health team daily as the change was implemented.

Linda had decided from the beginning to keep a daily diary and had been keeping meticulous records of nutrients and the medicines from the first day she met Ginger. She knew that she was fortunate that Ginger had been able to tolerate the changes. Ginger was an exceptionally cooperative patient. This was the only life she knew. She was now nine months old.

Adri had been just as diligent with the play therapy and developing Ginger's skills. Ginger was achieving on age level in all areas of motor development, and her cognitive development was that of a one-year-old. Ginger was laughing and loving life with her adoptive family.

Since Ginger was developing right on target and tolerating the changes in her formulas/medications, Cord, Adri, Ginger, Linda, and Marion resumed their travel schedule. They settled into their routines. Adri, Ginger, and Linda toured while Cord and Mario continued to make sales and advance technology. Ginger continued to gain weight and advance in all skill areas.

Everything was going well, and before they realized it, Ginger was turning one year old. This was a milestone for Ginger's Health Team. Ginger's next milestone would be at 18 months. Cord and Adri planned a day of fun and partying in the safest place on earth for Ginger, their home. They planned the day of partying with the four people who loved her most. Ginger loved being surrounded by her extended family. When Ginger laid down for a nap, they all dropped. Their faces were even sore because they had been doing so much laughing.

That night Cord and Adri had a serious discussion about Cord's business. They were both in agreement that Cord would train at least two presenters. He would start using them in the presentations, which was a part of his programs that he had always done since the creation of his programs. He wanted to eventually free his schedule and be able to focus on Ginger and her happiness.

Chapter 4

UNKNOWN TO LINDA, Marion planned an evening at Linda's favorite Mexican restaurant. Linda loved Mexican food. If she was asked where she wanted to eat, that was always her first choice. The owner of the restaurant was well aquatinted with Marion, Linda, Cord, Adri, and Ginger. Even though reservations were not required, Cord always called Mr. Cruz to let him know they would like reservations. They preferred a quiet cove on the enclosed Patio. It was the safest seating in order to protect Ginger.

Mr. Cruz would always open the patio side door and greet them personally. Adri would be carrying Ginger and Cord would be rolling Ginger's highchair. Cord had purchased an easy fold highchair with wheels. When it was folded, it took about as much room as a senior citizens walker. Cord's staff kept the highchair clean and sterile. The high chair had a specially made cover to maintain a clean, sterile environment. Anything Ginger's adopted family could think to do to for Ginger, they did. The chair was easily unfolded and locked in place.

Ginger did not eat any solid foods, she continued on a strict regimen of nutrients. The wonderful thing was Ginger showed no desire and had never experienced hunger. After she was placed in her highchair, Cord would fill her tray with toys and electronics. Cord continued to develop technology and games, especially designed for Ginger to encourage her skills development.

Today, Cord and his family had arrived ahead of Marion and Linda, just as Marion had planned. When Marion and Linda arrived, they were greeted by Mr., Cruz and escorted to their favorite alcove. Linda was pleasantly surprised to see Cord, Adri, and Ginger. There were hugs all around. Margaritas magically appeared. Marion turned to Linda and knelt on one knee. He produced a beautiful diamond ring and asked, "Linda, would you marry me." She quietly answered, "Yes." Marion placed the ring on Linda's hand. Linda was in awe, and the ring was a beautiful marquee diamond. It was obviously several carrots.

Adri immediately wanted to know what type of wedding Linda might want. Linda did not hesitate, and she said I would love to be married in your flower garden. I would like Ginger as my flower girl, and you and Cord to stand up with us. Everyone lifted their glasses in agreement. I have waited for My Marion since the day we met so I would like to marry in about two weeks when the flowers will all be blooming. Marion looked at Linda and said, "I'm beginning to doubt I surprised you with this engagement." Linda laughed and responded, "Today, you surprised me. That doesn't mean I haven't been envisioning our wedding for a long time".

Adri wanted to know about Linda's dress and what she and Ginger would wear. Linda was saying that she loved Ginger's and Adri's wardrobes and whatever Adri chose for them she knew would be perfect. Fajitas, Chili Rellenos, Quesadillas, all Linda's favorites were served with the Margaritas flowing. Everyone was celebrating, when Cord made a toast, "I want to make a toast to our dearest and closest friends, I feel we are one step closer to completing the circle of Ginger's Family." Everyone raised their glasses in agreement while Ginger clapped.

When they were finished celebrating, Mr. Cruz thanked Marion for choosing his place of business for this most important occasion. Mr. Cruz escorted them to the patio door where their limousine and driver awaited.

The celebration continued as the couples arrived home and went to their separate suites. Linda and Marion headed straight for their spa bath. While Cord and Adri put Ginger down for a nap in her crib and hurriedly stripped down and jumped each other in their bed.

After a night of lovemaking, Marion awoke and went to retrieve his briefcase. Linda awoke as soon she felt Marion leave the bed. Marion wanted Linda to know his net worth. He wanted Linda to have the wedding of her dreams, and he didn't want her to think she needed to scale down her wedding because they couldn't afford it. What he began showing Linda was the enormous amount of wealth he had accumulated. Linda assured him that she was getting the wedding of her dreams.

She also assured him that he didn't even need to ask her to sign a Prenuptial agreement. She would sign immediately. Marion assured her, there will be no prenuptial agreement. What I have is yours. "I love you with all my heart, and you are the only lady I want to spend the rest of my life with."

The next two weeks rushed by. As if by magic, the flowers in the garden bloomed and became more beautiful every day. Adri and Ginger went with Linda to shop for her wedding dress. Adri picked out three she thought might be perfect for Linda. Linda fell in love with the first. She didn't even try the other two.

The family minister and his wife were happy to reunite with the two couples. The minister counseled with Marion and Linda over the next two weeks. He was very impressed with their maturity and the genuine love he observed between them.

An Arbor of flowers was in full bloom so it was decided that the wedding party would stand under the Arbor during the service. On the day of the wedding, a Grand Piano magically appeared in the garden. Stacey would be playing the piano and singing during the ceremony. Stacey had a beautiful voice and was also a very gifted pianist.

As the wedding began, the minister escorted his wife through the garden and to the piano. Then he kissed his wife, and he went to stand under the Floral Arbor. Stacey began playing as Marion and Cord entered from a side path and stood under the Floral Arbor. As the music continued, Adri carrying Ginger came into view. Adri placed Ginger on the path with her flower girl basket filled with pedals from the variety of flowers in the garden. Ginger wobbled down the path tossing flower petals in the air. Adri followed closely. Everyone was laughing, including Ginger. Their dresses were beautifully embroidered with flowers matching all the varieties in the garden. Linda was thinking about how beautiful, and she couldn't imagine anything more perfect. Linda stood back and admired her wedding party, her best friends.

When her gaze settled on Marion, Stacey began playing the bridal march. She could not take her eyes off the handsome man that would soon be hers the rest of her life. She had never dreamed that her life would be so fulfilled. Marion was gazing back at Linda as intense, and he loved her so much. He knew they were destined for a very loving relationship. He also knew what a conscious and caring lady Linda was. He had seen her in action. He knew her values were not just talking. Linda was a lady of action, and he loved every aspect of her.

When Linda took Marion's hand, they turned to the minister, and he prayed a prayer of blessings on Marion and Linda and their extended family. Stacey then began singing and playing a lovely song of blessings. Marion and Linda were so moved by the song that they both had tears in their eyes when Stacey was finished singing.

Marion and Linda had both wanted a traditional ceremony, after reciting their vows and reading of scripture, the minister pronounced them husband and wife. He concluded you can now kiss the bride. Marion was kissing Linda when he heard a small voice saying my turn. Everyone laughed; it was Ginger's turn to kiss the bride.

A celebration catered by Mr. Cruz followed the ceremony. There was plenty of food and music.

Marion and Linda slipped away for a private celebration of their own. No one knew the details on where they were going on their honeymoon, but security knew it would have a spa tub and bathroom. With luxurious robes.

Chapter 5

WHEN MARION AND LINDA RETURNED, the house was under renovation. Cord and Adri had decided to renovate three rooms on the third floor. They were changing the windows and lighting, and we're going to introduce Ginger to every form of art, they could think of. They purchased finger paints, chalk, markers, crayons, with all textures of paper. In one room they introduced Duplos, tinker toys, Lincoln log, every shape, form, and color of blocks they could locate.

Ginger seemed to take to the finger painting the most, at first. She liked the texture to be very thick. Adri would dress her in white onesies. They kept the onesies in the room with the other art supplies. One day when Cord was watching Ginger, he got a call. He was watching Ginger when he saw her go to the cabinet and get another onesie. Before he could conclude his call, Ginger had taken out five onesies, laid them down on her worktable, and painted a different pattern on each. Cord took pictures and sent to Doug. Doug called immediately and asked to represent her. Cord was laughing so hard; Adri ran to see what was going on and had to take the phone and find out from Doug.

Doug could not get them to take him seriously for quite a while, then he said," Let me do this for our angel." Those were the magic words. Cord ran out and ordered onesies in a variety of sizes, and Ginger was happy to paint her visions on them. Doug decided that the original onesies done personally by Ginger would be priced upwards of $500. Doug had also set up production of duplicate designs that would be in retailers for $100.

The day of Ginger's First Style show was a huge success. When Doug told Cord and Adri, he planned on using one of his venues, a large venue. They both laughed, but this was Doug's area of expertise. The invitation went out. Cord and Adri knew what time to arrive with Ginger and they arrived at the side door as directed. Doug met Ginger, and she went happily with him.

When Doug returned with Ginger, she looked adorable. Doug said the photographers were ready in the front of the venue and Doug, Ginger, Cord, and Adri headed to the front of the Art Venue. Adri couldn't catch her breath when she saw the backdrop. It was so real! Ginger was in the center looking adorable in her painted white onesie, and the background dressed in his white coveralls was JP. Their hair was even styled the same. In the corner, there was a little stick angel (their trademark). The title of the show was "Art in Me." Doug waited for their reaction. They were deeply moved. Finally, they were quietly heard saying "perfect."

Doug's decisions proved right throughout the show. Hundreds are attending. Artist, Engineers, Friends of JP's, Doug's, KD's and Coree's. The Art in Me style show was a celebration of life. Colonel Wright attended and asked Adri for a minute with Ginger. She climbed into his lap, and he began, "I want to tell you a story about your Dad. When the Naval engineers were working on a problem they couldn't solve, I would find your Dad and your Uncle to help. One day I went to their workshop, and your Dad and Uncle were both working. Your Dad was dressed just like in that picture, white overalls with paint Splattered on him. Your uncle was dressed in denim overalls. The Engineers were on a deadline, so I didn't let your dad and his brother change clothes. There were a few new engineers in the department, and when I brought in your Dad and Uncle they said, "Who are these clowns, and why did you bring them here?" Your Dad and Uncle walked over to the desk they used turned up the light and started working. Within the hour, your Uncle KD said, "look at this." Your Dad said, "look at this." They exchanged drawings. Then your Dad took out a red nose and put it on your uncle and said, "It works." Then your uncle took out a red nose and put it on your Dad and said, "It works." They both honked the red noses and said, "Solved the problem. Not one way but two ways." Clowns Rule! I've kept those noses all this time, and I brought them tonight to give them to you. Your Dad was a very intelligent man and helped the Navy any time we ask".

Colonel Wright didn't tell the rest of the story only because Ginger was so young. But it just so happened that the Administrator of the hospital was in the building. As a joke, the new engineers told him there were two clowns in the Engineering

Department tonight that wanted to visit kids in the hospital. The hospital administrator went to the classroom with the Engineers. When he walked in, he recognized JP and KD, but he went along. He told them all the kids in the hospital were asleep. But JP told him well I'm having trouble making this disappear. It was a folded check. JP twirled it between his fingers and clapped his hands, but when he opened his hands, the check was still there. JP asks the hospital administrator if he could make it disappear. He opened the check and saw it was for $500,000. He said, "I'm sure I can make this disappear." But KD was not to be outdone by his older brother. He said, "He could not make this (another folded check) disappear. He rolled it between his fingers and twirled around three times and opened his hands. The check was still there. KD unfolded the check and said, "Can you make this disappear." The hospital administrator said, "Thank you JP and KD, the kids at the hospital will magically make these disappear. It turns our JP and KD were generous benefactors to the Post Hospital, and they had called the Hospital Administrator to meet them after Colonel Wright had picked them up that night. Clowns Rule!

The Colonel set alone and thought about JP and his generosity. He could tell Ginger one story after another, and maybe when she was older, he would get the chance. He thought what I want right now is a good cheeseburger and cheese fries with a 44oz Coke, and I know just where to get them.

'Art in Me" was a huge success. The onesie art sold out, and four major chain store placed orders. Many of the Stars present ordered original pieces. When ordering, you could request size and colors, but the vision was entirely Ginger's. By the time Ginger had completed the orders from the Style Show, she had moved onto another Art Project. The production continues to run the line, and they were sold out the next two seasons.

Adri was sitting in a chase watching Ginger with her Art Projects. Ginger started adding sand to her finger painting and Adri text Cord. "Got a chemical engineer in the making." Cord rushed up to see what Ginger was doing now". Ginger continues to mix house products with her paints and started making the pictures on canvas. (Mainly because the canvas was strong enough to hold the paint).

Ginger didn't need to generate money. JP had left her a fortune to last her natural lifetime. Cord and Adri supported Ginger's Art as a form of play. She was healthy, gaining weight, her developmental skills were on target or advanced, and most of all, Ginger was happy and having a good time.

Once Doug saw the Canvas Art Ginger was producing, he called Coree. Coree was very excited about the designs, textures, and colors that Ginger was using. He could see many of his clients, especially his commercial accounts, would have a real interest in her art. Coree contacted Cord about setting up an Art Show exhibiting Ginger's new pieces. Cord told Doug and Coree that Ginger had been making really large pieces lately, some pieces she continued from one background to the next to complete the whole composition. He sent current pictures. The art pieces were right in line with what Coree had in mind.

As before Doug took the lead. He wanted once again to use the stick angel as the trademark. This time he wanted to incorporate both JP and KD. He also maintained the name of the art exhibit, "The Art in Me." Doug felt strongly that this talented angel's Art Pieces were the best part of her Dad's and her Uncles Art visions. He knew he could feel JP was watching over his little angel. So many times, he looked at Gingers Art Work and saw how similar the strokes were or recognized a new color scheme that he thought JP would have loved.

Cord and Adri gave Ginger the freedom of her art. They never directed her to play. They never required her to complete a project. Her art was what she produced, and they made sure Doug and Coree agreed. They were happy to agree because of Ginger's talent they didn't need or want duplicate Art Work. They loved the one of a kind piece. When it was time for the Art Exhibit, Doug had used one of his venues, but for this show, he and Coree were more selective with the guest list. When the photographer arrived for the red carpet, Cord, Adri, Ginger, Doug, and Coree went to the Red Carpet Display. Doug had designed a backdrop that centered Adri in a white angel dress with realistic white wings and a halo. Up in the clouds were PJ on the upper right and KD in the upper left looking down on Ginger. The title "Art in Me." With a small Stick angel in the lower right. It was magnificent. This was Coree and Doug's World, and they knew it well. They brought in a guest that was competitive in bidding, and before the night was over, Ginger's Art Projects would be created and delivered around the World.

Ginger was healthy, and Adri and Cord were spending every day surrounding her with love. Adri was watching Ginger create when she felt she was getting a migraine. She told Ginger, then she went to get her medications. When she came back, she had put on a short white silk nightie. She had also brought a sheet to wrap herself in if she got too cold but usually being cool help. She laid down on a lounge chair. Ginger asks her Mother if she could rub her head to make her feel better.

Adri agreed, and Ginger's cold little hands felt so very good. Adri was getting drowsy from the medicine, but she kept telling Ginger how good her little hands felt. Adri notices the change but didn't question Ginger. It now felt like Ginger was putting a cool lotion on Adri, then she would rub it until it seemed just the right temperature. Adri went to sleep, and while she was sleeping Cord came in. Ginger said, "Mommy has a migraine." Cord asked, "Does Mommie know what you're doing"? Ginger answered, "Yes, Mommy said it made her feel better before she fell asleep." Cord immediately got the camera and started taking pictures. It was a high definition camera; they kept one in each Art room to document Ginger's Art.

When Ginger was finished, she moved on to something else. But Cord set close to Adri. Adri slept soundly. She hardly moved. Cord had paged Marion and Linda to get Ginger and clean her up and do their nightly routine. Linda and Marion loved it, as far as they were concerned, they never got enough of Ginger. Cord was thinking it was because of the pain pills that Adri lay so still. It was an hour and a half before Adri woke up and saw Cord watching her.

Adri saw Cord immediately, and she was smiling up at him when she realized she was too stiff to move. She was wondering how long she slept when Cord told her he had something for her to see. He picked up the camera and said, "Our daughter's masterpiece." Ginger had painted Adri from head to toe, and it was a very provocative piece of art. Cord said, "I wish I could keep you just like you are." Then he laughingly climbed on the lounge chair, and they made love.

They had paint all over both of them now. They went into the shower in the Art Room and made love again. Then they laughingly went to their Master Suite and ate Steak.

It did take Cord a little time only because he wanted complete confidentiality, but he found someone to develop and frame the pictures of his wife. He hung them in their bedroom.

Adri's interest turned to ride her low wheeler and later her bike. Cord and Marion set her up speedway in the gym. They bought her a Princess Car, a Bat Mobile, whatever she was interested in. Then one night after her bath, Ginger crawled in bed with her Mommy and Daddy. She kept pulling on her ear. Cord noticed, and Ginger said, "I think I have a migraine in my ear." Adri jumped up and got the thermometer. Ginger's temperature was 101. Cord called the doctor while Adri dressed. Linda and Marion brought the car around, and they met Ginger's doctor in the emergency Aides unit. Ginger's doctor seemed very calm. She took a test. It was an ear infection.

Now was the time for the doctor to decide on the antibiotic she should prescribe. She could not risk jeopardizing Ginger's immune system, but she needed to get rid of the infection as quickly as possible.

Ginger's team of health providers made the decision. Cord, Adri, Linda, and Marion stayed the night with Ginger at the hospital. The ear infection was responding to the antibiotics, and Ginger was released to go home.

That night in the hospital was harrowing. Everyone was trying to remain positive but heartbroken about how this would affect Ginger's future. Ginger was now two years old. The statistics showed, and they knew that every day they had from now on was a gift, a blessing. Cord had called and made arrangements for a cleaning team to go through the house. His staff was vigilant about keeping the house sterile, but Cord used a service from time to time. The service was comparative to a crime scene cleanup crew only they were trying to prevent a crime. They were trying to find the deadly germs that threatened their daughter.

Ginger was her happy and playful self and never realized the threat to her life. As far as she was concerned, she had a migraine like Mommy and Daddy and the next day, she felt better.

Within a couple of days, the family and extended family were back into their regular routine. Enjoying life and laughing with a two-year-old. When you think back on things, you always think, what could I have done differently. Would we have been more prepared if Ginger had shown signs of the serious infection that was attacking her? Every answer is, you never want your baby to suffer.

Ginger climbed in our bed and started cuddling. She said, "Mommy, you know I love you"! Adri said," Ginger, you know I love you," Then she said, "Daddy, you know I love you." Cord said, Ginger, you know I love you". Then both Cord and Adri smothered Ginger in kisses while she giggled. Then Ginger said, "I think I'm going to see JP tonight." "I think I am going to be your Guardian Angel." Adri could hardly speak. She asks, "Why do you think that"? "JP is my guardian angel, and he told me." Adri and Cord hugged Ginger tight, and they didn't want to let go. They finally all fell asleep. At 2 am, they woke up to find Ginger had passed away in her sleep. Pneumocystis Pneumonia, her killer.

And Stacy sang and played. Stacey said later it was the hardest thing she had ever done. Their minister knew Ginger well and talked about her many talents. Ginger had been so healthy. They had hoped and prayed for a miracle. It was a wonderful memorial service because of all the video of Ginger laughing at life. Laughing with her Mommy and Daddy, Laughing with her extended family.

Then the big screen lit up with Ginger's face, and she said, "Mommy, you know I love you." Adri said, "Ginger, you know I love you." Then she said, "Daddy, you know I love you." Cord said, "Ginger, you know I love you." Then both Cord and Adri smothered Ginger in kisses while she giggled. Then Ginger said, "I think I'm going to see JP tonight." "I think I am going to be your Guardian Angel." Adri could hardly speak. She asks, "Why do you think that"? "JP is my guardian angel, and he told me."

The video stopped, then the backdrop from Ginger's Art Exhibit dropped over the screen. There was Ginger dressed in white with wings of angels and JP and KD pictures in the clouds with the small trademark of a stick angel in the corner.

The minister read from Hebrews Chapter 13 verse 2. "Do not forget or neglect or refuse to extend hospitality to strangers, for through it some have entertained angels without knowing it".

Cord, Adri, and the whole household will never forget the sweet innocent Ginger and all their happy memories.